Mc

MW01231969

Mountain Laurell

A Novel

John Shivers

fairDALE
publications
Calhoun, GA

www.jshiverswriter.com
jswriter@bellsouth.net
Facebook: JShivers Wordweaver

Cover Art by Tracy McCoy

This book is a work of fiction. Names, characters, places and incidents either are the product of the author's imagination or are used fictitiously. Any resemblance to actual events, locales, or persons, living or dead, is coincidental and beyond the intent of either the author or the publisher.

Printed in the United States of America

ISBN: 979-8-6219037-3-2

Dedication

To… My grandchildren… Grant Lewis and Lillie Lewis. I love you both and I'm so proud of each of you.

To… Dianne VanderHorst… page layout professional, without whose great attention to detail, none of my books would ever see print. Thanks, Dianne!

To… Elizabeth, my wife and partner in this writing life who, when she gives herself a chance, has some talent with a paintbrush. She may not be in the same category as Laurell Wilson and Mary Elizabeth MacCallum, but MY Mary Elizabeth McCallum Shivers has earned the right, through eighteen books so far, to have a main character named for her. After all, we celebrated 50 years of marriage this past Valentine's Day. I love you, Elizabeth!

Other Books by John Shivers

Create My Soul Anew Trilogy
Hear My Cry
Paths of Judgment
Lift Up Mine Eyes

◊

Renew A Right Spirit Series
Broken Spirit
Merry Heart
His Mercy Endureth
Let Not Your Hearts Be Troubled

◊

Repossessed

◊

Slop Bucket Mystery Series
Boat Load of Trouble
Out of Thin Heir
For Sale... Or Not?

◊

Gone Astray

◊

Colorblind

◊

In Service

◊

The River Rolls On

◊

Christmas Collector **Series**
Three Gifts For Christmas
Weaving a Family for Christmas

AUTHOR'S NOTE

Long before I ever assumed the editorship of "Georgia Mountain Laurel" magazine in 2007, I'd already fallen in love with those pristine white blossoms with the wine red markings that bring the foothills of the Appalachian Mountains into full and beautiful bloom each spring. When the offer was made many years later for me to become editor of the magazine named for these mountain beauties, I found it both fitting and more than a little ironic.

It must have been along about 1995, give or take, that the idea for a book with the main character named Laurell – that's with two L's – visited me. I took the time to grab the premise of the story, and even wrote the first twenty or so pages. Then the file got put away, and out of sight, out of mind, I'd long since forgotten the story.

In 2019, as we were downsizing our home, I was tasked with going through boxes that had been sealed for some twenty years. While most of the contents were destined for the recycle center, I did come across the beginning of **Mountain Laurell**. It was like being reunited with a long-lost family relation, and included the small floppy disc that contained the file.

It took a little work to retrieve the contents of that disc, but once I was able to open the document, I discovered that the storyline still spoke to me. I'd just finished **The River Rolls On**, and instead of going on to the next book on my list, I began to finish the job I'd begun so many years ago. Now I give you: **Mountain Laurell**.

2020

Think about it…

When you buy a book from an author
you're buying more than a story.

You are buying numerous hours of errors and rewrites.

You are buying moments of frustration and
moments of sheer joy.

You are not buying just a book, you are buying something
they delight in sharing;

a piece of their heart, a piece of their soul…
a small piece of someone's life.

Chapter One

Her face flamed hot, like last summer's sunburn. It wasn't the first time she'd heard the cruel remarks people offered without being asked, even when she could hear them. If there was laughter in her vicinity, it was usually at her expense. This time, it was two old women in the corner who were making fun of her. Mountain folks weren't very friendly, or even tactful, when it came to dealing with strangers. She'd learned this early on. Now, almost a year later, she and her family were still very much the outsiders.

"To them," she whispered, as she struggled to hold her tongue, "we're known as the city folks over to the Justice place." If only they could understand why the city folks had to come to the mountains, it might make a difference. Then realizing the insanity of that thought, she made the snap decision that their neighbors didn't need to know all about the Wilson family. Or why this was literally their last chance.

"Young lady, do you want this or not? I'm not gonna stand here all day holding it." The voice that bit into her already bruised feelings belonged to the scarecrow's twin standing behind the counter. His oversize lens were so thick, the glasses perched atop his nose gave him the appearance of a big-eyed bird with vision problems. The brown paper sack in his hands was clutched almost protectively, almost as if he hoped she'd refuse it.

"What?" Where had she been? When she came back to the

present and re-connected with the storekeeper, Laurell had to wonder just how long she'd been standing there. "Oh, yes, Mr. Holland, I'm sorry. I was daydreaming." That wasn't exactly true. Her thoughts had been on the circumstances that had brought them to Hickory Bend, high in the North Carolina mountains. Which, she told herself, was much more like a nightmare.

But there was no sense letting the two old biddies know they'd gotten to her. She reached for the bag. "Thank you. Mama needs the flour and eggs to cook lunch."

The storekeeper still held on to the bag with her two purchases. "You got money for this?"

One of the biggest adjustments in their move from the Atlanta, Georgia area had been in the food-buying process. No longer could she just dash down to the supermarket. Twin Lakes General Merchandise was the only place within more than twenty-five miles to buy groceries. And overalls. And seed and grain and fertilizer and gasoline. Unlike the mega-market where Laurell had shopped for several years, in this store you told the grocer what you needed, and he gathered it for you.

"No, sir," she said. Laurell didn't understand why he was asking for payment. They always charged everything and her mother paid the bill monthly. "Just put it on our bill, and Mama will pay you at the first of the month, like always."

He shoved the bag across the counter, but still didn't totally relinquish contact with the brown-colored sack. "Well, you see," his voice, obviously affected by too many years of smoking, said, "that's the problem." He glanced at a huge calendar on the wall nearby. "It's now the ninth of the month, and she hasn't paid last month's bill yet. She knows she has to pay by the third." He examined Laurell so intently, she wondered for a moment if there were bugs crawling over her. "You folks having money problems or something?"

Caught off guard, Laurell didn't know how to respond. Money had never been flush, and following her father's death, much of what they'd had suddenly disappeared. That's why they'd had to move to the mountains. Well, that and Russell's problems. That was why they'd had to do a lot of things that were unpleasant and distasteful. Some of it had been personally heartbreaking for her.

"I don't know," she said finally, unsure of how to respond. For certain, she knew she couldn't pay for the supplies Mama needed. She had no money in her purse, which was nothing new.

It's not like there's anything here to spend money for. Wouldn't matter if I had a bundle.

"Well, you tell your mama this is the last thing I'll charge until she brings me some money." He gazed at her with such intensity, Laurell felt like she was shrinking right before his eyes. "You tell her to bring me some money and talk to me, you hear girl?"

At that moment, groceries or not, she just wanted out of that store. "Yessir, Mr. Holland. I'll tell her. Just as soon as I get back."

And I will!

Fearful if she hesitated any longer, that he might change his mind, she grabbed her purchase and beat a hasty retreat. The heat of embarrassment consumed her entire body, and Laurell wondered if she could ever look the storekeeper in the face again. Every time she turned around, it seemed, something else had been robbed from her. This time it was her dignity. Again.

As she made her way toward the double screen doors and freedom, the two old women were still discussing the city folks. She had already learned enough about mountain ways to know that Mr. Holland's harsh words would furnish them with gossip material for the next month. What's more, they made no effort to keep her from hearing their vicious remarks.

"Knowed from the git-go that Wilson woman wouldn't be able to make it with that bed and breakfast place." The voice belonged to the taller of the two ladies, and her words had made their way around the wad of tobacco clutched tightly in her left cheek. "Havin' money problems, they are. Nobody with good sense ever come here, and everbody here is hankering to git out."

"Wonder how much longer they'll last?" the other woman said. "They ain't hardly had nobody staying there these last few weeks. Know what I'm talkin' about." She preened with self-anointed importance, and seemed to get taller right before Laurell's eyes. "I keeps my eyes open, I do."

It was obvious that she would have to pass the two women to make her exit, and they didn't make it easy. Laurell knew she was trapped, but the true extent of that trap was much deeper than the current humiliation. She'd been trapped since the day the moving van had set down their furniture at Oak Hill House. What's more, it was a trap she saw no way to escape.

"My boy, Elmer, he left here the day after he quit school, an' I don't hardly see him no more," the woman with the chew of tobacco said. "Iffen somebody who's been here all they lives can't make it, I don't git how these city people with they big ideas thinks they can. She and her young'uns oughta stayed where they was." Her sermon

14

finished, the woman stamped her foot, and a stream of tobacco juice arched toward the base of old wood stove, where it appeared many before her had used the tin safety liner as a makeshift spittoon.

"Heered tell they ain't got nobody else," her gossip companion said. "They desperate."

"Then they didn' need to come here," the first woman said, as she adjusted the wad in her mouth. "We don' need 'em and I don' know of nobody else that wants 'em here."

Laurell had heard all she was willing to tolerate. Picking up the pace, she sailed within inches of the two women. Her head was up and her nose was in the air. Suddenly, she didn't care if she got the label of snooty. They both knew she'd heard everything they said. No defense she might mount would resolve the problem. Nothing would make a difference, because, as she suddenly understood, they should have stayed in Atlanta. They would always be outsiders here in this mountain community. Nothing she could say to them would change the way she and her family were perceived.

Mama, however, was another matter. Laurell picked up her pace for the two mile walk home, vowing to have a serious conversation with her mother as soon as she got there. Never mind that lunch preparations were underway. This was more important, and Mama would simply have to listen. She wasn't famous for being understanding. Daddy had always said it came from managing close to two hundred people. When you have that much responsibility, you couldn't afford to be too approachable. Otherwise, people would take advantage.

Unfortunately, her daddy had also said, Mama didn't know how to leave that side of herself at work. So when she would get on a tirade with one of them and come off as unreasonable, Daddy called her hand. He was the only one who could manage her, and now he was gone. It'd been Laurell who'd been placed in the unfair position of having to combat her. After she was widowed, her emotions had become even more brittle. That's also when she'd begun to favor her son over Laurell.

I feel almost like a traitor, even thinking these thoughts. But truth is truth. If anything, Mama's much more rigid than she was before Daddy died, and we had to leave Atlanta. This is all going nowhere good.

After the semi-darkness of the old country store, the early May sunlight was brilliant and blinding. In her haste to get away, Laurell stumbled into the road, caught herself to keep from falling, and headed toward home. Unfortunately, the word home automatically conjured images of the comfortable, sprawling, middle-class house in one of the Atlanta suburbs, where she'd lived for more than seventeen years. She didn't know if she would ever be able to consider the old, two-story lodge where she now went to bed each night, as her home. Even after all this time, it still felt like she was squatting, uninvited, in someone else's house.

Like it or not - this near foreign substitute for home was her destination, and the climbing temperature, if nothing else, was impetus enough to encourage her not to dawdle. Eighty-eight, the old Coca-Cola® thermometer on the porch at the store had proclaimed. Mama needed the supplies and she needed to talk with her mother. As she made her way up the winding, two-lane road, perspiration began to run off her in rivulets.

"This day's gonna be hotter than a fire ant convention," she announced to the world at large, then immediately realized what she'd said.

"Fire ant convention, indeed," she muttered, chiding herself for the slip of the tongue. She might not be accepted by the natives, but she was certainly beginning to adopt their speech patterns. "I need help badly."

Finally the lodge came into view, and Laurell halted her uphill trek to rest a minute and gather her thoughts. She'd covered the distance from town in record time, if you could call a general store, a post office, and the public fishing dock a town.

"I've had about all of the ridicule I'm going to take from a bunch of ignorant hillbillies. We just have to go back to Atlanta." As she made her way down the drive, she knew that even going back to Atlanta wouldn't mean everything would be like it had been before. Daddy would still be dead, and their beautiful home was now owned by someone else. "I don't care where we have to live, as long as we're away from here."

Racing up the back steps two at a time, Laurell was a young woman on a mission. She let the heavy old screened door bang shut behind her. Better to carry out that mission while her anger was high and her nerve was up. Mother, she knew, could be formidable when she wanted to be.

"I've seen that side of her more and more in the past eighteen months. Especially where I'm concerned." She was talking to herself, she realized, but shoved aside the fear that someone might overhear.

"Mama? Mama?" She looked around the kitchen as she deposited on the big center island the supplies in the "paper poke" she'd learned the mountain people called grocery bags. "Are you in the house?" Sometimes she would spend time caring for the flowers around the house, but Laurell knew she hadn't seen her mother on the grounds. Hearing no response, she made her way until she arrived at the foot of the big staircase to the second floor.

"Mama? Are you here?"

"Up here." A voice floated down from overhead. Laurell assumed her mother was holed up in the little office she'd constructed out of a large closet shortly after they'd moved in. "Did you get what I needed from the store?"

"In the kitchen," she said, "but I need to talk to you." Then feeling that she hadn't adequately communicated how serious the conversation was, she added, "Now."

A head appeared over the upstairs banister railing. "Now? Can't it wait?" Laurell noticed how her mother's mouth was crooked upward on the left side.

Uh-oh. I've seen that expression before. Something's got her upset.

"You don't know what kind of morning I've had." Her mother's voice was rising by decibels. "Whatever it is, I'm sure it can keep until after lunch." She descended to the main level in a slow, studied manner that Laurell also recognized. From experience, she knew her mother's body language was screaming, "Don't mess with me."

Laurell decided to take the hint. So much for her determination to make her mother listen to reason. Not that she'd ever listened before. "You're right," she said, "it isn't that important." She put her arm around her mother and felt the tremble that coursed through her parent's body. "It can keep until we do the lunch dishes." She steered her mother toward the kitchen. "Now, what do I need to do to help you with lunch?"

While bed-and-breakfast operations don't usually serve a lunch meal, Laurell knew her mother had decided to offer a noon meal, for an additional cost, to their guests, and to any of the public who might stop in to eat. With no other food service establishments within easy driving distance, they usually ended up feeding a small crowd most days.

Her mother had put chickens in to roast earlier in the morning. Now Laurell moved into place and began to tackle the various tasks necessary to produce a meal. There was little conversation, because none was necessary. Each of them knew her role, and together, they made it happen.

We make a good team, Laurell thought.

As she washed salad makings, Laurell's mind once again replayed the events that had brought them almost three hundred miles from home. Before Dad had died, her mother had been the executive assistant manager of a five-star hotel in downtown Atlanta.

They'd been a two-person team then, too. How she wished they'd been a good enough team that it hadn't been necessary to move. She knew it hadn't been easy for Myra to trade a great desk job with good pay and benefits, for the role of mountain innkeeper. While her mother had had all the administrative skills needed to run a hospitality business, Laurell understood that in her new job, she'd been confronted with tasks she'd never encountered at the luxury hotel. Jobs like fixing leaks and unstopping toilets, and cooking for crowds.

No one could have been more shocked than Laurell was when her mother's announcement had ripped her entire life apart. They were moving to the Appalachian Mountains it seemed, where a distant cousin owned a white-elephant piece of property he hadn't been able to unload.

Laurell wondered if that shouldn't have told them something, but she was fearful to say so.

"We don't have much of a choice," Mama had said at supper that fateful night. "Dad made good money, but we spent good money. He had life insurance, but unless we start living out of that account, we've got to sell this house and downsize. We can't make it on my salary alone."

Laurell had been born at Atlanta's Northside Hospital, had grown up in the house on Peach Orchard Lane, and had expected to stay in Atlanta for the rest of her life. Surely she would marry someone from Atlanta, and they would grow old there together. Suddenly, that perfect scenario was beginning to shatter.

"We can get an apartment in April's complex," she offered. "I'd like that."

April was her best friend, and she and her divorced mother lived together in a really great apartment. It would be nice to be just a few doors apart. Without paying any attention to the look on her mother's face, Laurell waxed on.

"They make it really well there, and April even has a window seat in her bedroom. And they have a real fireplace. You know how you've always wished we could build a fire on cold winter evenings."

She was just rattling on, totally caught up in the beautiful picture emerging in her mind, when she caught sight of the grief-stricken expression on her mother's face. The next words she heard confirmed the worst.

"Don't you understand? We can't even afford to move to April's complex. I'd like that, too, but money is going to be very tight."

Suddenly the lifestyle she'd envisioned exploded in front of her eyes. What could her mother be talking about? "Then what're we going to do?"

Mama didn't back up from explaining what they were going to do, Laurell reflected later. To say that Laurell had been horrified was an understatement. "We'll sell the house and leave Atlanta. We'll go somewhere that we can live more economically," Mama said.

"But Mama," Laurell had protested, "what about your job? If money's so short, how can you quit your job? We'll just have to live close enough for you to be able to get to work." She recalled a movie she'd seen a few months before, during her senior year of high school, where an unfortunate family lived out of their car. The prospect made her blood run cold.

"Surely you're not suggesting we'll have to live in the car? We'll at least have to trade for a bigger model to have room for you and Russell and me." She tried to make a joke out of her question, but there was no feeling of humor behind it. At that point, it wouldn't have surprised her if that was exactly what her mother had in mind.

Is she having emotional problems? Has Dad's death finally taken its toll? Laurell couldn't help but wonder.

One thing that Laurell couldn't bring herself to consider was that her own plans, revolving around classes at one of the south's premiere art colleges right there in Atlanta, might be impacted. If they moved very far away, how would she get to school? She'd already been accepted and had won a partial scholarship. It was to be the start of a wonderful journey toward her goal of becoming a serious artist.

"You're right, we can't live in the car," her mother said, and Laurell dragged herself back from the pity party she was already hosting. "I have a place that would combine home and work, and would totally eliminate the need to commute." She hesitated, grinned, then continued. "Sort of like we'd be living over the store."

Laurell could tell that her mother was uncomfortable, and that made two of them.

"In fact, we'd hardly need a car, and that would make my car that was new last year last a lot longer."

Laurell couldn't believe what she was hearing. "You're opening a store? What do we know about running a store?"

"Not a store," her mother said quickly, by way of correction. "A bed-and-breakfast inn."

"Bed and breakfast?" Laurell was familiar with the concept. Seeing how it could all work was another matter entirely. And how far out of Atlanta would this be?

The suspense couldn't be denied any longer. Laurell finally gave voice to the main question that was haunting her. "But Mama, what about me? What about art college?

The look on her mother's face spoke volumes before her mouth ever moved. Laurell saw actual tears in Myra's eyes, and it took everything she had to keep her seat. What she really wanted to do was bolt and run, as far away and as fast as possible.

"I'm so sorry, hon. Even with your scholarship, we couldn't swing the remaining tuition, if we did stay here." She reached for Laurell's hand, but in a childish moment, her daughter withdrew her hand, even as she withdrew into herself. "Besides, where we'll be, it wouldn't even be practical for you to commute to class."

Where we'll be. What is she talking about?

Almost as if she hadn't even noticed that her daughter had checked out, Myra Wilson continued to explain. Laurell realized that she was missing something important. It was only after they'd finished the conversation that she was able to put two and two together to understand all that her mother had explained.

Her plan, it seemed, was to purchase a lodge deep in the mountains in North Carolina.

"It was my cousin's parents' mountain home. They're dead, but they used to host big house parties. This house was built for entertaining. Your Dad and I went to one of their shindigs when you and Russell were both little. You kids stayed with your grandparents. It's got twelve bedrooms and all but two of them have a private bath. That would give each of us a room, and leave us nine rooms to rent."

Laurell was desperate to derail this train that threatened to take her away from everything that was precious.

"It's a beautiful place," Myra waxed on. "You'll absolutely love it."

How can I love anything that takes me away from Atlanta, my friends, especially April, and my one chance to become a professional artist? This is so unfair. Oh, Daddy, why did you have to leave us?

"But Mama," she'd found the words to protest, "that place can't be cheap. How can we afford it? Wouldn't it be better to rent something here and you keep your job?"

"That's the beautiful part about this. Roger, my cousin, doesn't want the house, and so far, he hasn't been able to sell it."

"And you still think you should buy it?"

She spoke to Laurell as if she was a kindergartener. "He'll make me a great deal, plus he'll finance it for ten years. We wouldn't have to touch very much of what we get for this house to make this happen."

Laurell could tell that her mother was totally sold on the game plan she'd just laid out. Desperation caused her to play the one card she hoped would throw a monkey wrench. "What about Russell, Mom? What are you going to do about him?"

Russell was her brother, two years younger, who'd already been in minor trouble with the law. His bad judgment had only been acerbated after their dad's sudden death. Laurell knew her mother was very worried about him.

"That's why I wanted to talk to you tonight," Myra said, "while he's still at ball practice. We need to talk to him together."

She knows he's not going to buy this idea, Laurell told herself. But how could she help sell him on moving, when she didn't even accept it herself?

"Mama," she said, searching frantically for the right words, knowing she might only have the one chance. "Russell is not going to like this. I think we'd better figure out a Plan B."

"But I can't see any other way. This isn't a piece of cake for me either. I'm having to give up my job and future promotions, as well as my friends." Her voice halted, and Laurell suspected she heard a sob in her mother's voice. "We absolutely cannot stay here," she said so softly Laurell had to strain to hear.

Laurell said, "He'll be home any minute. Let's put this on hold and you and I can talk about it again tomorrow." *If only, somehow, I can buy a little time.*

She was desperate to devise a way to keep them in Atlanta. Perhaps if she slept on it, she counseled herself, something would come to her.

"All right," her mother said. "I've got a few days before I have to give Roger a check for the down payment. We can talk more tomorrow."

She wasn't home free and clear, but nevertheless, Laurell breathed a giant sigh of relief. At least nothing had been done that couldn't be undone. She was just beginning to enjoy the piece of homemade apple pie her mother had served for dessert, when the doorbell rang. She and her mother looked at each other, the same unspoken question hanging between them.

"I'll get it," Laurell volunteered. She jumped from her chair and headed for the front door, with no idea who was on the other side. Still, she was shocked to find two blue-uniformed officers. Between them, looking very pale and uncomfortable, was her brother, squirming where he stood. She didn't need his body language to tell her that this was bad.

"Good evening, ma'am," one of the officers said. "Is one of your parents home?"

Mountain Laurell

Chapter Two

Kitchen clean-up after the lunch rush was delayed, and then it was delayed again. Their lunch trade had been better than usual, but the down-side was that both Laurell and her mother had to keep moving to get everyone served in a reasonable time. Their lunch meals had proven very popular and most profitable. One disgruntled customer could ruin everything. Too much was riding on the word-of-mouth reviews they got.

When the last customer had departed, after enthusing over the tasty meal she'd enjoyed and the generous portions, Laurell had hurried to lock the front door. She was already losing her nerve to share the storekeeper's words from earlier that day with her mother. Nevertheless, it was something that had to happen. And it would have to happen that day. There would probably be something else they'd need tomorrow, but Mr. Holland had made it clear. Nothing else could be charged until he received payment for what was already owed. It was something that Mama simply had to deal with.

Hot water was running in the sinks and Laurell was stacking all the dirty pans in one place near the washing side. She'd already loaded the twin dishwashers with cutlery and china. If they didn't get the kitchen in order pretty quickly, it interfered with preparation of the evening appetizers for that night's guests, and making the yeast breads that would be served at breakfast the next morning. For a rare change, they had six rooms already reserved for that evening and the next, and it wasn't uncommon for an occasional walk-in customer to boost their occupancy numbers.

"Mama! I'm ready to start washing," she called aloud. She and her mother always did the heavy washing together, and were able to put things to rights pretty quickly. Where can she be?

As she was about to begin the chore by herself, the memory of the phone ringing as the last few diners were finishing their meals came to her. She remembered seeing her mother leave the dining room to answer the call in the kitchen. But she'd never come out. Although, obviously, she was no longer in the kitchen. Before she got her hands wet, Laurell reached for the wall phone nearby, and quietly lifted the receiver. The sound of Myra's voice assured her of her mother's whereabouts, but the frantic conversation she overheard did nothing to reassure her. It was wrong to eavesdrop, she knew, but the panic so evident in Myra's voice compelled her to keep her ear glued to the phone.

"I'm telling you," she heard her mother say, "I've dealt with it. He's made amends and I don't intend to be harassed over this. He's said he was sorry, and I've paid for the damages. Now get off this phone and leave me alone."

Laurell felt she'd been sucker-punched. The "he" her mother referred to could only be her brother. But what had Russell done now? She wasn't aware of anything lately. In fact, her mother had commented only a few weeks before that her brother appeared to finally be coming around. Now…? If her mother's panicked words on the phone were any indication, that didn't seem to be the case.

She glanced at the clock, noted that they should already have been finished with the cooking utensils, but not even the first pan had been washed. She plunged her hands into the soapy water and began scrubbing.

"Laurell? Where are you?"

The words were coming from upstairs. "I'm washing pots and pans. We're behind." She continued working down through the stack. "Mama? How soon are you coming down? Remember, I need to talk to you."

"Oh, honey, I'm sorry. In all the rush, I forgot. And now I've got a major headache. I've simply got to lie down."

Laurell gritted her teeth, tempted to abandon the task, because by that time, she had a headache of her own.

"Can you finish the kitchen and prepare the finger foods for this afternoon's reception? I'll make the bread when I come down later."

"But Mom," she said, struggling to keep the anger that threatened to erupt out of her voice, "we HAVE to talk, and we have to do it now."

"Darling, I'm sorry, but my head is killing me. Can't it wait until later this evening?" Without even waiting for an answer, Laurell heard her mother's parting words. "I'm sure it can wait."

All I am is a maid, a kitchen helper, an errand-runner, and a whipping boy. Meanwhile, Russell doesn't lift a hand to do anything around here, and he gets away with murder.

The thought of all her brother's transgressions reminded her again of the conversation she'd just overheard. Was that the cause of her mother's sudden headache? She'd been fine before the phone call came.

What can he have done now? As her mind ran the gambit of all his prior offenses, many of which had drawn the attention of the police, she remembered again, back in Atlanta, the night the police had brought him home. She relived the nightmare that resulted, and all the grief it had caused.

I had to give up my friends, but more importantly, my education, and my plans for the future.

Mama had tried to pacify her by promising that once they were settled, a way would be found for her to begin art lessons again. But it had been almost a year, and it seemed that there was no one nearby who even painted. There was no one to teach a most-talented young woman, who'd been forced to give up everything. Even if that qualified teacher did exist, there never seemed to be enough money ahead to pay for the lessons.

No money for lessons and no money for groceries. I wonder how much longer there'll be money to keep us here? And when it runs out, where will we go?

Memories of the night Russell had been brought home under arrest were still crystal clear all these months later. He'd been caught in the act of selling some marijuana and prescription pills. Where he'd gotten his inventory, nobody knew and he'd refused to provide his source. In fact, Laurell remembered, he'd been downright belligerent toward the both of them, as well as the two officers that had brought him home.

"Ma'am," one of the policemen had told her mother, "you better be glad this boy is still younger than sixteen and will be dealt with as a minor. Otherwise, he'd be staring at twenty years in prison, and depending on how compassionate the juvenile court is, he still may have to do some time."

The prospect that her baby might have to serve jail time, and that he was mere days away from his sixteenth birthday, had spurred her mother on to get them out of Atlanta. The promise to talk further about the prospect of moving to North Carolina had fallen by the wayside. The very next morning, before she even began shopping for an attorney to defend Russell, she'd had her bank wire the down payment on the lodge, and it was a done deal.

Thanks to a very good, but over-priced attorney, and Russell's sham behavior of throwing himself on the mercy of the court and pretending to be contrite, leniency was granted. Minutes before going before the judge, he'd popped off several times about how he was going to tell the court they could stuff it, if they thought he was going to stand still for kangaroo justice.

His mother had appeared incapable of reining him in. It was Laurell who'd grabbed him by the scruff of the neck and said, "If you don't shut your ignorant mouth and understand what's at stake here, I'm going to tell the judge what an arrogant liar you are and beg him to send you to jail."

Laurell felt rather than heard the gasp her mother uttered in reaction. "Laurell, don't say that. We're all stressed over this. Now, apologize to your brother."

But Laurell had dug in her heels. "Mother, I will not apologize for telling the truth." She regarded her brother with a searing look that he actually had the decency to acknowledge and drop his eyes. "If he doesn't lose that attitude, I will do exactly what I threatened."

Whether it'd been her strong words or the fit of conscience Russell suddenly seemed to experience, she didn't know. But when she and her mother finally accompanied him out of the courtroom, he'd managed to escape by the skin of his teeth.

"Two years' probation," the judge had ruled, along with a fine of two thousand dollars, and forfeiture of Russell's newly-minted driver's license. Any further infraction of the law, in any way, would result in immediate confinement in jail. When the attorney had explained that Mrs. Wilson was due to move the family to North Carolina within the next two weeks, meaning that supervised probation would be difficult, the sentence suddenly changed.

"In that case," the judge said, looking intently at the defendant's mother, "if you're taking him out of Georgia, then there'll be no probation. But don't bring him back into the state for at least two years, or I'll have to reinstate the probation."

In other words, he's North Carolina's problem, and now because of his stupidity, we can't come back to Georgia to live. How is that fair?

Laurell had thought the situation was bad enough, but to her surprise, it got worse. The latest insult came down the next morning, shortly after the real estate agent, who was listing their house for sale, left with signed contract in hand.

"I've got some bad news for you," Mama had said, after she'd bid the agent farewell along with the promise that they would be out of the house within ten days. "I'll have it professionally cleaned," she'd promised.

"What is it now?" Laurell braced herself. "What do I need to do to be ready for the movers?" She looked around and realized she hadn't seen her brother that morning. "Where's Russell? He needs to be helping."

"I've just gotten the quote on deep-cleaning this house," her mother had said. "Between that expense and Russell's court costs and the fine, there's not going to be money for your long-distance learning courses from the art school." Laurell was certain that she saw tears in her mother's eyes, but suddenly they were far too little, way too late. "Maybe in a few months?"

That promise definitely had a question mark on it!

"But you promised…!" she said between gasps of disbelief. "I was counting on this." It felt so dirty to beg, but Laurell couldn't shut up. "When I agreed to give up my scholarship, you promised I could go to school online."

After conversation with the school, when Laurell had been forced to withdraw before she even got started and had to relinquish her scholarship, the possibility of going to school online had been offered to her. It hadn't been her first choice, but she'd quickly decided it was better than nothing. And it promised to be much less expensive than taking courses on campus.

Laurell had held her breath when she laid out the plan to her mother, who had quickly agreed that they could manage to make it happen. Only now, she was going back on her word.

"But… but… but that's not fair," she practically screamed. "One more time the juvenile delinquent is getting everything he wants, and I'm being shortchanged."

Unable to shoulder the disappointment and the bitter taste

her mother's announcement had deposited in her mouth, Laurell had left the house on a dead run. When she finally arrived home from spending the day with her friend April, it had been a stressful evening with little said by either party. Russell, on the other hand, had been most vocal on his thoughts about his sentence.

"When we get to North Carolina," he'd crowed, "I don't have to sweat stupid fuzz or probation officers or retarded judges. I'm home free."

"This is a chance for you to make a new beginning," Mama had said. "I hope you make the most out of this opportunity."

Yeah, the opportunity I'm paying through the nose to buy for you, Laurell had thought.

In the end, she'd finally apologized to her mother for her outburst, but she'd refused to apologize for feeling that she'd been treated badly. And she'd threatened her brother within an inch of his life, if he didn't straighten up once they got to their new home.

Russell had to ride the bus to the county comprehensive high school twenty miles from the B&B, where he was in his junior year. It was, he'd informed their mother after the first day, greatly beneath his dignity to have to share a common school bus with hillbilly children.

"They're all stupid," he'd declared. "They're nothing like me, so you're either going to have to drive me back and forth, or let me drive the car." From the way his face glowed when he proposed driving back and forth to school, Laurell understood that her brother had very carefully structured his solution to the problem.

"Right," she'd said, before her mother could respond. "You want to put two hundred miles a week on our one car, just because you're too good to ride the school bus. Have you lost your mind?"

"Now, Laurell," Myra had said, her hands fluttering as she tried to mediate the situation. "Please don't be so harsh with your brother."

Laurell had done a slow burn and had to bite her tongue, before she'd said, "Mama, it's past time for Russell to learn that the entire world doesn't revolve around him. When he wears out the car because of his refusal to do what thousands of students do every day, how are we going to replace it? You make me walk to the store to keep from using the car."

Myra had chewed her lower lip, continued to flap her hands, and said nothing.

"Besides," Laurel said, "how's he going to drive without a license? Even if his license hadn't been lifted, it would be a Georgia license."

It was obvious from the expression on the faces of both mother and son that neither of them had considered that aspect.

"I can get my North Carolina license," he'd informed her with a smirk on his face. "I don't need the Georgia license."

Laurell wasn't sure if what she was about to say was accurate, but if it derailed her brother's pie-in-the-sky plans, even for a little while, it was worth the chance.

"Good luck with that," she said. "North Carolina will check other state databases to see if you have a license in force. When they find out your Georgia license has been suspended, even temporarily, there's no way you'll get a North Carolina license." Then a second point came to her. "And even if you could get the license, our insurance won't cover you until the judge says you can drive again."

The plume of steam that raced to the top of her brother's head and seemed to form a mushroom cloud over him, was a good indication of how her words had hit home.

He whirled on his heels to confront their mother. "Is that true, Mom? Does Laurell know what she's talking about?"

Indecision was written all over Myra's face, while Laurell held her breath, wondering if once again, her mother was going to pull the rug out from under her. "I suspect she's right," she said finally. When her son's face clouded up, she was quick to reach for his hand, as she said, "Besides, son, we really can't afford the gasoline or the wear and tear on the car to go back and forth every day."

He hadn't liked it, but the next morning, Russell caught the bus at the end of their driveway, and the matter wasn't spoken of again. However, neither had Russell wholeheartedly taken advantage of the second chance. His grades were marginal at best, despite their mother's pleas for him to apply himself. More troubling was the appearance of friends from school, who had suddenly begun frequenting the inn, collecting Russell and bringing him back at all hours of the night.

They look like scum of the earth!

Laurell and her mother had exchanged words about the situation more than once, with her mother inclined to grant him leniency and liberty. Laurell thought they were playing with fire that would burn them both badly later, if not sooner.

Slowly, over time, the police began to visit the B&B. Russell had skipped school. Russell and some of his friends had been caught in a bar in Asheville, were underage and belligerent. One of the boys that Russell ran around with was caught doing ninety in a fifty-five mile zone, but it had been her brother who had read the traffic officer the riot act.

As far as they knew, he wasn't involved with drugs again, although Laurell had her doubts if he was as clean as her mother preferred to believe. What's more, every time the police brought him home, Myra worried that word of his actions would get back to the judge in Georgia. Laurell believed it was only a matter of time before the court found out the rest of the story.

I don't know how I'm going to deal with Mama if he gets sent off to juvenile detention. She will absolutely freak. She knew that her mother's emotional reaction would be targeted at the judge, and not her son, whose own actions had landed him in trouble. *It's not like he hasn't been warned, repeatedly. He may have to hit rock bottom to ever see reason.*

Now it appeared that her brother had other transgressions that she knew nothing about. It was clear that her mother was playing with something that could blow up in her face. And now the storekeeper had threatened to close their account unless he was paid.

Could whatever Mama paid to the person on the phone, to make amends for Russell's actions, be the reason she hasn't paid Mr. Holland?

Suddenly, it was more urgent than ever that she and her mother have a conversation. However, it wasn't to be, until after the front door was locked that night, and after all their guests had retired to their rooms.

"I'm going to bed," Myra said, as she extinguished some of the lights on the main level. "I'm exhausted and five o'clock will come before I'm ready."

Later, Laurell would wonder where she'd found the wherewithal to confront her mother, but the realization that the important conversation was about to get deferred yet again, caused her mouth to seize control.

"No, Mama, you're not going to bed just yet. I'm sorry you're tired; I am, too. But we have a matter that has to be corrected first thing tomorrow morning. So sit down and listen."

As Laurell related that morning's conversation with the storekeeper, omitting the comments of the two women in the store at the same time, the highly-excited color in her mother's face drained out to a sickly white.

"Tell me the truth. Did you forget to write that check, or do we not have the money to pay Mr. Holland?"

The expression on her mother's face answered the question faster, and more accurately, than any words could have conveyed. Suddenly Laurell's anger that she'd been innocently caught in the middle with the store owner propelled her to be much more pointed than would normally have been her bent.

"Has Russell done something else? Have you had to spend money to get him out of trouble? Otherwise, why didn't you have the money to pay the grocery tab?"

Suddenly, I feel like I've become the parent and she's become the child. How did this happen?

"Tell me, Mama," she insisted. "If you didn't spend the money on Russell, why haven't you been able to pay the bill? Don't you understand… if we need something tomorrow morning when we're cooking lunch, he won't charge it to us? In fact, he said for you to come see him and bring him his money."

They had been standing in the foyer, beside the door. Myra reached behind her and her hand came in contact with a chair. Seemingly out of starch, she collapsed, as she waved her hand. It appeared she was asking for time. As impatient as Laurell was to get to the bottom of the problem, she held her tongue.

With her eyes cast to the floor, Myra finally mumbled in such a low voice that her daughter had to lean in to make sure she heard correctly. "Russell shoplifted some merchandise in an electronics shop and got caught. When he saw he was in trouble, he dropped what he'd stolen and it broke."

That stupid idiot. Has he lost his mind? Now he's stealing!

"He fed the shop owner a line about his daddy being dead and us being up against things financially." Myra ran her hands through her hair, creating a most unkempt result. "It was a husband- and-wife shop, and the husband was gone when the wife caught Russell. She fell for his guilt trip and promised they wouldn't press charges, if we paid for what he took."

The memory of her mother making a sudden trip to the county seat a week or so before made instant sense. "That's why you went into Meadeville the other afternoon? To pay Russell out of trouble. Again, Mother. Again."

"I know, you're right. But I simply can't abide the thought of him being in jail. So, yes, I went to pay what they demanded. And I thought it was over, except it took most of the money I had earmarked for Mr. Holland."

"So why did those people call at lunch today? That was who you were talking to when you didn't come downstairs to help me wash up."

Fortunately, Laurel told herself later, her mother was so scattered, she didn't think to question how her daughter knew about that conversation.

"That was the husband. He says his wife shouldn't have listened to Russell, and should have called the police and had him arrested. Even though I paid for everything, he's still threatening to have him picked up. I don't have the money to pay a fine or hire an attorney."

"I can't believe we're having this conversation," Laurell said at last, unsure of what else to say. "You shouldn't spend any more money on getting him out of trouble. It doesn't matter whether we've got it or not."

She placed her hands on her hips, bit back the words she really wanted to say, and instead observed, "Russell is totally out of control, Mother. If you truly love him, the only way you can rein him in is to let him fall and pay the price."

Almost as if she hadn't heard Laurell's words, Myra said, "But thanks to our good occupancy rate tonight, you can pay Mr. Holland in full. There's a list on the refrigerator of what we need tomorrow."

Laurell couldn't believe what she was hearing. Her mother expected her to deal with the grocer and make everything right.

"Sorry, Mama," she said. "I'm not going to do your dirty work this time. Mr. Holland was very specific. He wants to see you, so if you want this matter handled, you're going to have to do it yourself."

With that, she turned on her heel and climbed the stairs, feeling her mother's eyes boring into her back. Once she was behind the closed door of her bedroom, it all became too overwhelming. Sobs consumed her as she collapsed on her bed.

Is there no end to what Mama expects me to do for her? How much more do I have to sacrifice?

Chapter Three

W hen they met in the kitchen the next morning, no mention was made of the previous evening's exchange. Neither were they their usual chatty team getting breakfast on the buffet for their guests. Since neither mother nor daughter was truly a morning person, the easy give-and-take that usually punctuated their breakfast-making tasks made working half-asleep all the more tolerable. This morning, however, Laurell had felt herself most resentful that she had to sacrifice her sleep.

The temptation to boycott her kitchen duties was almost overwhelming. But it was a B&B, and that second B stood for breakfast. It wouldn't do to lose customers because the breakfast didn't live up to expectations. With a lousy attitude, she reported for KP duty.

When the kitchen was put to rights, Myra said, "There's the list on the refrigerator. I've added a couple of things. See if you see anything I've forgotten while I go change clothes."

Evidently she's going to the store. I refuse to ask.

When her mother descended to the main level a few minutes later, the dread of what she was about to do was written all over her. Just watching her made Laurell hurt, but she couldn't find it within herself to give the woman a get-out-of-jail-free card. Mama was the one who wasted the grocery money, and Mr. Holland had specifically said, "You tell her to bring me some money and talk to me, you hear, girl?"

That's how it would have to be.

Myra headed toward the door, put her hand on the knob, hesitated, then finally said, "Won't you at least go with me? I'll do all the talking, but at least go with me to give me moral support."

Laurell's heart tore as a result of her mother's pleading words. "All right," she said, "I'll go. But you'll have to let me change first."

This is the woman who managed a staff of two hundred and met conflict head-on?

She wasn't surprised when Myra indicated that they would take the car.

It's okay for Mama to ride to the store, but I have to walk.

Once they were in the store, where several other customers moved about in different parts of the big one-room shopping center, it was clear that Myra expected Laurell to stand with her when she spoke with the storekeeper. Instead, Laurel took herself to the farthest reaches, where she couldn't even see Mr. Holland and her mother.

As she was browsing, making the deliberate decision not to even look the other way, she stumbled across an older woman squatted down in the hardware section, digging in a big lazy-susan Christmas-tree-looking contraption. Large bins, five levels of them, encircled what would have been the trunk, and each layer was smaller than the layer below. Each bin held a quantity of nails and screws. The woman, who looked almost like a homeless street person if they'd been in Atlanta, looked up as Laurell approached. The expression on her face was one of utter shock.

Laurel saw the woman's body language reaction, but didn't understand what had triggered it. What's more, she didn't know what to do to make amends.

"I'm sorry, ma'am, I didn't mean to startle you."

The woman said nothing, but quickly jumped to her feet and left the area, even though it appeared she hadn't found what she'd sought.

Before she could decide whether to be insulted or sympathetic, her mother approached.

"Mr. Holland is getting our order together. It'll be put on the account."

She acts like it was nothing. I don't get this.

"I've got to get back to the inn. If people are calling for reservations, there's no one there to book them." She rewarded her daughter with a wide smile that indicated it had all been much ado about nothing. "Can you wait for the order to be ready and bring it home? That way we won't have to burn gas again today. Plus one of us has to get started on lunch."

You're going to ride home in air-conditioned comfort and I'm going to have to walk carrying groceries again.

She mentally reviewed the list that had been posted on the refrigerator and decided there was nothing heavy enough to cause problems. And her mother was right: if lunch preparation didn't begin very soon, they wouldn't be ready to serve at eleven-thirty when they put out the OPEN sign.

"Go on home," she said at last. "I'll be there as soon as I can."

As she wandered around the store, glancing toward the storekeeper every little bit, as if she could somehow hurry him along, she kept thinking about the elderly woman she'd surprised earlier. As best she could tell, the woman had departed the store. But who was she? Laurell was confident she'd never seen the woman before, and she'd been in the store almost every day for the past year. Her imagination was working overtime, trying to create a scenario that would explain everything.

"Got you ready," the merchant called out. "Miss Wilson, here's your order." His gaze was much softer and more tolerant than it had been the day before. As she approached the counter, he slid a ticket across with a pen laying on it. "Just give me your signature and you're good to go. I appreciate your business."

Evidently they got everything worked out.

Laurell signed where he'd indicated and picked up the order, which he'd put into a brown cardboard box that had once held jars of prune juice. She couldn't help making a face when she realized what had come in the box.

An idea occurred to her. Before she had time to talk herself into keeping her curiosity to herself, she said, "When we got here, there was an older woman over there." She pointed to the corner of the store, where she had seen the mysterious customer, and did her best to describe her. "Do you know who she is? I've never seen her before and we've been here more than a year."

Mr. Holland didn't hesitate. "You must be talking about Mary Elizabeth MacCallum. She's lived around these parts for about as long as I have."

Laurell's curiosity was running full tilt. "Then why haven't I ever seen her? And why did she act so skittish? All I did was walk up; I didn't even seen her at first, and she ran like a scared rabbit."

"Imagine she did," Mr. Holland said. "She's more or less a recluse. Lives back in the woods in a little log cabin. Last time I saw her before this morning was more than a month ago."

A recluse? Sounds like there's a story there.

"Why does she hide out?" A troubling thought hit her. "She's not wanted by the law or anything, is she?"

Mr. Holland chuckled. "Not hardly. You must read too many of them mystery books." His expression changed. "Nope, she lost her daughter in a very tragic way many years ago. She's never been the same since."

"Oh, that's so sad."

Laurell meant the words. She was about to ask for details, when the phone on the counter between them rang. Mr. Holland reached for the receiver as he said, "See you your next trip in. And tell your mama I'm sorry your brother's been sick and she had medical bills."

Laurell's lower jaw dropped and for a moment, she'd questioned if she's heard correctly.

"I admire any woman who can raise children by herself. Just tell her next time to talk to me before she's late, and there won't be no problem." He turned to take the call, and Laurell heard him say, "Twin Lakes General Merchandise."

Yep, she had heard very correctly.

Mother told him that Russell's been sick and that's why she couldn't pay our bill. As far as I'm concerned, he is sick. But I'm the only one who really believes that. So now she's doing the very same thing he did at that store, where he stole that stuff. Try as she might, she couldn't excuse her mother's actions.

As she made her way up the road in the direction of the B&B, Laurell allowed her senses to indulge themselves. The morning was warm, but not uncomfortable. Not yet, anyway. Sunlight was in abundance and the sky was pristine blue, not a cloud in sight. Birds were singing in the trees and as her eyes lifted upward, she caught sight of the wave of receding mountains that cradled the little valley town. In a rippling effect, the green of the forests morphed into grey-green-blue hues, as the ancient hills got farther and farther away.

It was an artist's perfect subject. However…

I'd never even been in the mountains before we moved here. This wouldn't be a half-bad place if I hadn't had to give up my dreams and come here against my wishes.

The toot of a car horn passing startled her enough to bring Laurell back from her daydreaming. Without realizing it, she'd set the box of provisions down on the ground and had been rubbernecking. She glanced at her watch. She hadn't recognized the driver, but since she hadn't made any friends, she couldn't explain the greeting. But she could thank them. It was past time for lunch preparation to be in full swing.

"Oh, my, gosh. I've got to get home," she announced to the world at large, picked up her box, and struck out on a run. At least as fast as someone could run juggling groceries.

It wasn't until they were cleaning up the kitchen after another hectic lunch seating, that Laurell got the chance to say what her soul told her had to be said. Ever since her communion with nature on the way back from town, she'd felt the creative urges that hadn't surfaced since before they left Atlanta. In all the time that she'd been in the mountains, there had been no urgency to paint. Inspiration had lain dormant, and on those rare occasions when she thought about it, she'd wondered if it was gone forever.

But now she had the urgent need to hold a paint brush and feel at one with it.

"I want some time off," she said, as she and her mother were reshelving the cooking pans on the big, open-wire shelving units in the walk-in pantry off the kitchen.

She realized that she'd caught Myra by surprise, because the speed with which her mother jerked around to look at her daughter, and the expression of sheer panic on her face, told the story better than any answer ever could.

"Time off? What do you mean? How am I supposed to run this inn without you?" The woman was literally babbling, the words tumbling out of her mouth like the mountain river waters Laurell had seen alongside the road on the way to the county seat. "How much time are we talking about? Where are you going?"

She'd done this wrong. The subject should have been broached differently, although it did occur to her that at almost twenty, she could, and probably should, begin making a life for herself. But her more immediate task had to be to get her mother calmed. She held up her hand stop-sign fashion.

"Time out, Mama. Hold it." With her hand still in the air, she waited until her mother had ceased talking. "I'm not going anywhere. But I need a few hours a day, away from here, for me."

"But how can I do everything by myself?"

The true nature of her mother's problem was suddenly very clear. In her previous employment, Myra had been an administrator, with a staff working under her. She had made sure that their jobs were done, but she hadn't actually done the work herself.

This explains so much. Why didn't I see this before now?

Understanding, however, didn't change the situation. She plunged ahead. "I want a few hours a couple of times a week where I can paint. I'm not deserting you, although we do need to look around for someone we could hire to help out from time to time. What would you do if I was sick?"

"Don't even say that," her mother replied, and the panic was back in her voice. "Besides, how are we going to pay somebody else? We can barely pay ourselves."

She may be feeding and housing me, but so far, I've never seen the first dollar that could be considered pay.

"If we have money to pay for all of Russell's bad judgment, then we definitely have money to hire another pair of hands." She was immediately ashamed of her words. Well, maybe not the sentiments expressed, but the way in which she'd said them.

But in this case, I'm not going to apologize. She needs to hear the truth. I feel like this whole operation is on my shoulders.

From the color that infused Myra's face, Laurell understood

that her mother had gotten the message. What she would do with it was another matter entirely. Still, Laurell vowed, she would have time for herself.

If her mother was going to abdicate more than her fair share of the operation of the inn to her, Laurell would begin to function that way. "I'll begin making inquiries tomorrow about someone we can hire. And new employee or not, a week from today, I plan to take the morning off."

She looked intently to see how Myra had received that edict, and was saddened to see that instead of motivating her, it only seemed to further depress her willingness to fight.

What has happened to Mama? Oh, Daddy, I miss you so much. Why did you have to leave us?

If her father was still alive, Laurell knew, Russell wouldn't be allowed to run wild, and Mama wouldn't be struggling to keep everything together. What's more, Daddy would have seen to it that she accepted the scholarship and went to art school. At the very least, she assured herself, he would have supported her demand for some private time just for herself.

The remainder of the day flew by. Laurell and her mother went through the motions of getting ready for their guests, but the atmosphere of stress that had first shown itself when she'd proclaimed her intent to take personal time, persisted. There was just an undercurrent that screamed discontent on Myra's part. The next morning's breakfast load was heavier than normal, and for a while, Laurell struggled with whether she should wave the white flag and beg her mother's forgiveness.

While she dithered over what to do, the demands of the morning gave her no opportunity to make any overtures toward reconciliation. By the time the kitchen was put to rights and lunch preparation begun, Laurell was convinced that her mother would simply have to get over her snit. To emphasize that position, as soon as she could get to the mercantile, she posted the HELP WANTED notice she'd written out the night before. Mama had given her a short shopping list, and while Mr. Holland collected her order, she'd roamed the store. In the back of her mind, she'd been hoping to encounter the woman she'd seen the previous day.

"Got you ready to go," the storekeeper announced. "You have a good day."

I could have a better day if I didn't have to go back to the inn. What I wouldn't give just to be able to walk in the woods for a couple of hours.

"Thank you," she said, as she picked up the brown paper sack. She'd learned early on that Mr. Holland had no use for throw-away plastic bags like the big stores in Atlanta had used. As he'd explained the day Laurell had asked for "plastic instead of paper," you could always reuse paper bags in a number of different ways. Plastic bags, he'd insisted, were only good for one thing.

She left the store headed back to the B&B to help get lunch on the table. Her mother had gotten an excellent buy on some round tables with lazy-susans in the middle. They served the food family-style, which had seemed to be very popular with their guests. There were many people who drove several miles at least twice a week to enjoy lunch at Oak Hill House. At one point, when Laurell stuck her head into the dining room to see which serving dishes needed refilling, she'd decided that the crowd was larger than she'd ever seen.

That larger-than-usual lunch trade also translated into many more dishes to wash, and getting everything back in place ran into mid-afternoon. Laurell was as limp as the wet, used dish towels she'd hung on the rod next to the sink. It had been one more day, and she prayed that she could at least get an hour alone in her room to catch her breath. As she took care of the last few details in the kitchen, the phone rang. When her mother hadn't answered after the fifth ring, Laurell jumped for the receiver. She couldn't know it then, but that telephone call was about to make a big difference in their lives.

"Oak Hill House B&B," she said into the mouthpiece, hoping that her voice didn't exhibit the true depth of her exhaustion. "This is Laurell. How may I help you?"

She was expecting either a request to make a reservation, or a question about their lunch service. Instead, the heavy voice of a male, a voice that she didn't recognize, said, "I'm calling for Myra Wilson. This is a matter of some urgency."

"Just a moment, please. She's here, but I'm going to have to search for her. Will you hold, please?" Then another idea hit. "Or to make it easier on you, just give me your name and number and she'll return your call."

"I don't mind holding," he said, and the tone of his voice told her it was futile to try to persuade him otherwise.

"Then let me find her for you." Their phone system didn't have a call-holding feature, so she had no choice but to lay the receiver on the end of the counter, while she went in search of her mother. Thank goodness there were no other people in the house who might come through and hang up the receiver.

After calling and looking downstairs, she finally found her mother in her bedroom lying down. Her eyes were closed, and a wet cloth was across her forehead, but Laurell knew she had to wake her.

"Mama? Sorry to disturb you, but you've got a phone call."

Myra opened her eyes, removed the cloth, and raised herself up on one elbow. "Not now," she said. "Who is it? Just tell them I can't talk right now. Get their number and I'll return their call later."

"I offered to have you call him back, but he's holding. Said it was urgent."

With little patience, Myra threw the damp cloth aside, finished sitting up, and made to rise. "I'll get it in my office," she said. "Don't hang up downstairs until you hear my voice."

Laurell hurried back to the kitchen, grabbed the phone and said, "She'll be picking up in just a second." As soon as she heard Myra identify herself, Laurell made to hang up the phone. Her actions weren't fast enough, however, because the words she heard compelled her to continue to eavesdrop.

"Mrs. Wilson," she heard the man's voice say, "do you have a son named Russell Wilson?"

A sharp intake of breath threatened to reveal Laurell's presence on the line.

Oh, my, gosh. What has that jerk done now? This is getting ridiculous. She should have quietly hung up the phone, but with little shame, Laurell continued to listen.

"Yes, yes I do," Mama said. Laurell could hear the caution in her voice. "Who is this please?"

"Detective Teddy Bowman," the man's voice said. "Meadeville Police Department."

Oh, no. He's really done something.

The muffled sob she heard over the phone told her that her mother shared the same fear.

"Do you know where your son is?" the man asked.

Laurell glanced at the clock. Three-thirteen, it proclaimed. He should be getting on the bus to head home. He was usually home by four o'clock. He was complaining last night that it seemed like school would never be out.

"If he's not on the bus on his way home from school, he will be in the next few minutes." Mama hesitated. "Can you tell me what this is about?"

"For starters, Mrs. Wilson, Russell isn't on his way home. He went to school this morning, from all we can determine, but he didn't stay there."

"But… but Officer, there must be some mistake."

Laurell couldn't help it. Her eyes rolled into her head. Talk about an understatement.

"I'm afraid not," the officer said. "He was caught red-handed."

Uh-oh…

"I'm afraid I don't understand."

"Mrs. Wilson, you need to come to the police department as soon as you can. And you might want to bring your son some toiletries, because he'll need to brush his teeth here tonight."

This is so not good!

"What do you mean...?" Myra's voice dissolved into sobs. Finally she said, "Please tell me what's going on here."

"Your son was caught by the owner of Computers Plus trying to walk out of the store with a monitor."

Computers Plus. That's the place where he was caught shoplifting. Has he lost his mind? Why would he go back there?

After a long silence, Laurell heard her mother say, "I'll be there within the hour." Defeat and confusion were prominent in her voice. "Tell him I'm on my way."

Laurell made quick work of replacing the phone receiver as soon as she heard the click indicating that the other two parties had ended the call. It wouldn't do to be caught still holding the phone when her mother came downstairs.

In just minutes, Myra was in the downstairs foyer. "I know you were listening in, so I won't waste time telling you what's happened."

Laurell knew that she should be ashamed and should probably offer an apology. But if her mother expected that, she gave no indication. Laurell decided to say nothing.

"I need you to go with me," Myra said. "But I probably won't be back in time to greet our guests and get them checked in. So you'll have to stay and take care of them. We really can't afford to have anyone upset."

Myra didn't wait for an answer but made her departure, leaving her daughter to handle everything.

Back in the kitchen, Laurell made quick work of creating simple appetizers. This wasn't the time to tackle anything complicated. Hopefully no one would realize they'd been shortchanged. By the time she had the morning breads mixed and rising, it was time to wash her hands, straighten her hair and make-up, and be up front. According to the clock, it was time for the hordes to descend.

That's how I feel some evenings. Too many of these people think you ought to put them on a pedestal and cater to their needs only.

The entire time she was straightening registration forms and checking that the front steps had been swept clean of leaves, part of her mind was on what might be happening at the police station. She checked the clock for the umpteenth time. *Mama should definitely be there by now.* She tried to feel some compassion for her mother, but couldn't make it happen. So much of what was going on with Russell could have been prevented.

When the phone rang, it startled her. Certain that it was her mother, she hurried to grab it.

"What's happening…"

"Excuse me?" The voice was female, but it definitely wasn't her mother.

Ooops.

"I'm sorry," she said. "Oak Hill House B&B."

"You advertised for help," the unknown voice said, and her

words weren't in the form of a question.

"That's right," Laurell said. "Are you interested in the job?"

"Wouldn't be calling if I wasn't. I'll see you at ten-thirty tomorrow morning and we'll talk about it." The loud click she heard next told her the caller had hung up.

Laurell was left staring at the phone, and didn't have a clue what had just happened.

She didn't even give me her name. I guess we'll just have to wait and see.

Chapter Four

It was well after ten o'clock that night before Myra returned. She was alone, and gave every indication of total defeat, if the slump in her stance and the hangdog expression gave an accurate report. When Laurell questioned her, she just shook her head, while more tears appeared in her eyes. Eyes that looked like they'd already shed generous waterworks.

"I've got to be back in the morning at nine o'clock for his court appearance and hope that the attorney I've hired can get him out on bail." The tears turned loose in earnest. "Oh, Laurell, he's so pathetic. We've just got to get him out of that horrible jail."

"He should be pathetic," Laurell said, before her brain could govern her mouth. "As many warning signs as he's had, he's smart enough to figure out that you don't break the law."

Then, as her mind replayed what her mother had just said, two things suddenly stood out.

Attorney. Bail. Both of those equate to money.

She had to ask. It would incite her mother's anger, she knew, but she had to ask. "And just how are we paying for this attorney and how much is bail going to cost?"

"What's it matter?" her mother asked, and the quizzical expression on her face only underscored her confusion. "Your brother cannot stay in that jail. It's inhumane."

Anger shot up Laurell's back, and while she knew she shouldn't, the words exploded from her mouth with venom dripping.

"He made his bed, he can just lie in it." She began to pace the small foyer area, unable to remain calm, wishing desperately she could just start walking and never come back. "Mama, we don't have the money to keep paying him out of trouble. Did you not learn anything when Mr. Holland threatened to close our account?"

"But he's your brother. My child. If it was you in there, I'd be moving heaven and earth to get you out."

Well in the first place, I wouldn't be in there. I've got better sense. But I truly wonder if you'd actually be that forgiving with me?

"If you keep coming to his rescue, he'll never take responsibility for his actions." Her thoughts cycled back to the money. "But whether he deserves it or not, we don't have the money." Then she remembered the mysterious woman who was coming to interview.

"Besides, I've got a potential extra pair of hands coming here at ten-thirty tomorrow. For sure I can't hire her, if you're going to take what little we've got and squander it on an unrepentant juvenile delinquent."

The color rising from the shoulders in Myra's face slowly assumed a deep plum hue.

"Oh, my, gosh, Mama. Russell's seventeen now, almost eighteen," Laurell said. "Is he still considered a juvenile?"

Her mother's waterworks sprang back into action. "He's not," she said finally, after she'd grabbed a tissue and regained some composure. "The lawyer says he can do jail time for sure."

Laurell knew it would sound heartless. Or would it be realistic? Either way, she said, "He's obviously guilty. He was caught red-handed. If he's going to do jail time anyway, don't bail him out. He'll get credit for the time he serves before he's sentenced."

And we can save that money.

With a look that Laurell interpreted as total defection, Myra turned on her heel and rushed up the stairs. The young woman who was locking the door and double-checking the security system heard the sound of a slammed door and knew, once again, that Mama had buried her head deeply in the sand.

So much for trying to solve this problem with reason.

When she came to the kitchen the next morning, nothing was underway for breakfast. Normally by the time she got there, the lights were on, coffee was already making, the ovens were heating to bake the fresh bread, and various containers were spread out, ready to receive the scrambled eggs and breakfast casserole. On this morning, she'd turned on the lights, and a quick assessment told her it was going to be a very hectic morning.

Does she not understand that we have all our rooms rented? That's fifteen people total. Not counting us.

Hoping against hope that her mother was simply running behind, Laurell began with the basics, her eyes repeatedly straying to the doorway, anxious to see her mother standing there. By the time she'd had to accept, like it or not, that she was on her own, there wasn't time to dash upstairs to check.

She'll get here when she gets here. But that doesn't mean that I like it.

Because she knew she had no other choice, Laurell had the breakfast offerings set mere seconds before the first guest descended into the dining room. Over the next few minutes, one after another drifted in, while she replenished dishes and platters.

Man, these folks can eat. How long has it been since they've had a meal? Locusts wouldn't leave it this clean.

She'd removed all the emptied serving platters to the kitchen, and was gathering up the soiled china and flatware, when her mother finally put in an appearance. But appearance was an understatement. Myra Wilson looked as if a team of stylists had been at work. Laurell's mouth dropped.

"Do you think I'll impress the judge when I plead for bail for Russell?"

"Do you really think throwing yourself at him is the way to get what you want? And where were you this morning? Do you realize that I had no help with breakfast?"

Myra glanced around the room, almost as if she was seeing it for the first time. A smile played about her mouth. "It appears that you handled it beautifully. I knew I could count on you." She twirled as if to show off her butter yellow sleeveless dress, and seemed to delight in the image she saw in her own mind. She pulled out a chair and settled herself at the table.

"Will you bring me some breakfast? I can't face this ordeal on an empty stomach."

She actually expects me to wait on her and serve her. After she deserted me this morning just assuming that breakfast would happen.

"What, you can't go in the kitchen and serve your own plate?"

"Darling," Myra said, and the derisive tone of her voice was reminiscent of how a teacher would deal with a student who couldn't grasp that two and two equaled four. "You don't expect me to take a chance of getting something on my clothes, do you?"

The slow burn that was already smoldering suddenly flamed up. Laurell swung through the door into the kitchen, grabbed a clean plate, and began dishing up the breakfast leftovers. She barreled back into the dining room and slammed the plate in front of her mother, who rewarded her with a troubled expression.

"Laurell, you really need to work on your attitude. It isn't very pretty, you know." She forked into her breakfast casserole. "Oh, darling. You forgot my tea."

What? She couldn't even pour her own tea while I was getting her food?

She turned around to the sideboard, not three feet from where her mother was already attacking her breakfast, grabbed a cup, and drew a piping hot cup of the Earl Grey tea that was her mother's particular favorite. Mama had always acted like she was the queen. It had served her well in her administrative roles in a major hospitality company, but it had gotten old at home. In fact, it was old right now. Daddy would have called her on it. Except he wasn't there. However, right at that moment, Laurell was too exhausted to find starch for the fight she knew would result.

Myra finished her meal, detoured into the downstairs powder

room, and sailed by on her way out the door.

"Hold down the fort, dear. I know I won't be back in time for lunch, but you can handle it. And when I come home this afternoon, we'll have your brother back with us. I just feel it in my bones."

"You expect me to prepare all the lunch and serve it. By myself?"

"You can do it with one hand tied behind your back. You've got it nailed."

"Then I'm going to hire the woman who's coming to interview this morning, and if she can start today, I'll put her to work."

Laurel saw the troubled look crossed Myra's face, almost like she had an acute case of indigestion. She hesitated with her hand against the door facing. "I'm afraid we can't afford anyone right now, darling. It's all I can do to pay us. I don't know what I'm going to have to spend in court today."

But you've never paid me a dime for all the work I do!

The volcano was very close to blowing. So close, Laurell was trembling to control the threatened explosion.

"Let me get this straight, I'm supposed to work here day in and out with no pay and no help, just so you can continue to bail out a boy who needs to learn the hard way, that this world isn't beholden to him?"

"Dear, you really need to do something about all that bitterness you're nursing. It isn't pretty and it isn't acceptable. Now I have to run. Judges don't like you to be late to court, or so I've been told." Her declaration was punctuated by a titter. "You just need to develop some patience. We can make do for a little longer, and maybe in another month, we can afford to bring somebody on." She leveled an extended finger at Laurell's face. "You can do this."

With that, she was gone in a blaze of sunlight. From where Laurell stood, however, right at that moment, things looked anything but bright and promising.

She is exactly right. I do need to do something about my attitude. Only what I'd like to do isn't what she's recommending.

With no other choice, she grabbed the last of the breakfast debris from the dining room and adjourned to the kitchen, where she had to take stock and decide how to have both lunch and the inn ready for their guests on time. After all, what choice did she have?

The menu planned for that day required too much prep for one person, so Laurell made an executive decision. After a quick check of the pantry and the freezer, she came up with three different casseroles that would go together quickly and bake, while she worked on the salads. For dessert, she would make a quick version of peach cobbler and apple cobbler. If Mama didn't approve, tough!

She left me here by myself, and told me to handle it. Well, I'm handling it. Honestly, Mama will probably have more of a problem than our customers will.

Laurell was up to her elbows, literally, assembling the final casserole, when the front doorbell rang. Her grandmother, who had taught her much about cooking, had always maintained that the best mixing tools in the kitchen were those at the ends of your arms. Laurell much preferred that method herself, although she always heeded the warning to be sure her hands were clean. When the bell sounded, her first inclination was to ignore it. After all, she was busy. And she couldn't do everything, even though there were those who seemed to think otherwise.

"Yoo-hoo?" she heard a voice calling. "Is anybody here?"

She was turning a deaf ear to the summons, when suddenly it hit her. Oh... oh... the woman interviewing for the job. She pulled her hands out of the potato casserole mixture and hurried to the sink.

"I'll be right there," she called in the direction of the door and prayed the woman could hear her. As soon as she hands were clean and dry, she headed toward the foyer.

Standing on the other side of the door was a woman whose hair was four different colors. Four very vivid colors, braided and wound around her head, making it difficult to determine how old she might be.

"Augusta Corkern here," she said, as her hand shot out. "I'm ready to go to work." She pushed her way into the foyer. "Nice place you got here." Her head was almost swiveling three hundred sixty degrees, as she took in everything that could be seen from where she stood. She looked around again, then pointed off to her right. "I'll bet the kitchen's right through there." She made to head in that direction.

Laurell was still so off-balance from the whirlwind that was one Augusta Corkern, she couldn't find the words or the means to keep the person from taking over. Instead, she had little choice but to follow in the woman's wake. She had to figure out some way to fire someone who thought she had a job, and get her out of the B&B. There was still lunch to finish.

"Look, Mrs. Corkern," she said, as the kitchen door swung

shut behind them.

"It's Miss Corkern," her visitor informed her in a most imperial manner. "I've never been stupid enough to tie myself to any man."

Laurell ignored the information overload and said, "I'm afraid we've got a problem, Miss Corkern."

"You can say that again, Missy. You're seriously preparing food in here." She looked around again, and Laurell saw the woman's nose rise as her expression hardened. "This place ain't big enough to cuss a cat in," she said. "I can't work in close quarters. Claustrophobia, don't you know."

As the woman talked, and Laurell was able to study her more closely, she'd finally come to the conclusion that Augusta Corkern was in her early fifties.

"This is all we've got," she said in answer to the woman's criticisms. "But I understand about your fear of small spaces." She reached for Augusta's elbow, intending to escort her back to the door. The woman jerked her arm out of the way.

"But I can make do," she said. "Ain't never run away from a job, yet." A third glance around the now messy kitchen elicited another judgment call. "From the looks of things, this is a job. You need somebody bad. I could have done been here if I'd knowed there was a job waiting."

The woman was looking for a place to put the suitcase-sized purse that hung from her arm. Laurell knew if Augusta Corkern got any farther into their lives, they would never get rid of her. As badly as she needed help, she also knew that Miss Corkern wasn't it. They didn't have the money to pay her, and that was that.

"I'm sorry…"

"Oh, you don't owe me no apology. You can't help it you ain't got much of a kitchen. I'll make it work."

Desperation consumed Laurell, and she struggled to find a way to get rid of a woman who was fast becoming a pest.

There's no way I could work with her. She's way too bossy.

"Well, before you get comfortable here, I need to tell you. We can't pay you for working. Not yet, anyway. But maybe in a few weeks." She was rewarded with the woman whirling on her substantial heel, and the expression she wore would have been hilarious, had Laurell not been in a tight spot.

"You can't pay me? Then why did you waste my time bringing me here today? Do I look like I do charity work?"

"Look, Miss Corkern, when I posted the job, I didn't expect an immediate response. But more than that, you didn't give me a chance yesterday to tell you anything. You didn't even give me your name."

In truth, when she'd talked with the woman the day before, she hadn't known that Russell would throw yet another monkey wrench into the operation. But Miss Corkern didn't need to know that.

"Well, I never. I heared things was bad here, but I didn't believe it." The multi-haired woman hitched her purse higher on her shoulder, and strode toward the foyer, the heels of her shoes pounding out a tattoo on the hardwood floors. When she reached the door and fairly wrenched it open, she hesitated, turned, and rewarded Laurell with a look suggestive of deadly daggers. Laurell found the woman's eyes more than a little intimidating.

"When you get to where you can pay, do me a favor. Don't call me." With that, she sailed out the door and down the steps, to where a decrepit Toyota of as many colors as its owner's hair waited in the drive. The next sound Laurell heard was the car slinging gravel, as it roared out of the drive, followed by the peal of the kitchen smoke detector.

Oh. My. Gosh!

Fortunately the casserole was just a little overdone on top. It would still serve, she decided. There was neither time nor the ingredients to mix another one. Grandmother Wilson had also believed that a little carbon was good for a body. Laurell just hoped her customers shared Grandmother's philosophy.

Despite her best exhaustive efforts, it was a good ten minutes past opening time, before she was able to hide the closed sign and unlock the door. By that point, more than a dozen diners were already waiting, patiently, she hoped, for serving to begin.

By the time the last customer had left in the wake of compliments on the chicken and rice casserole, Laurell had to admit that everything had gone well, if you didn't count exhaustion. She'd heard no complaints, and she'd been on her feet constantly, replenishing dishes and refilling tea glasses, taking payments and fielding comments from her diners.

I did it, Mama. No thanks to you, I did it. But I can't do it again any time soon.

It was a gigantic relief to throw the door lock and turn out the OPEN sign. Laurell wanted nothing more than to retreat to her bedroom to sleep for the rest of the day. She also knew if she gave in to her exhaustion, she wouldn't get up again that day. *I'm just that tired.*

By detouring into the kitchen, she was able to bypass the stairs to the second level, and thereby ignore the urge to escape. Instead, she tackled the mountain of dirty pans and utensils, and when she finally placed the last pot back on its hanging hook, Laurell knew she had no other options. Her body was going to revolt if she didn't get off her feet, at least for a few minutes. But she'd sit in the great room downstairs and not go to the second floor. That way, she wouldn't be tempted to pile down on her bed. The recliner where she stretched out had never been more comfortable.

That's where she was when the door opened and Myra entered. Closely on her heels was an obviously angry Russell.

"You sold me out!" he screamed. "I told you I didn't intend to be held prisoner in this backwoods jail you call a bed and breakfast. And what do you do? You agree to play warden and let them put this shackle on me." His hand made stabbing motions toward his feet.

"Listen, son…"

"No, Mother. You listen. I don't intend to stay here any longer than I have to, and if you think I'm going to let this ugly piece of jewelry keep me here, you're crazy."

Laurell jumped from her chair and put herself in front of her brother, her arms raised in the standard time-out stance.

"What's going on here?" She looked from her mother to her brother, waiting for one of them to answer.

"He doesn't understand…" Myra began.

"She doesn't get it..." Russell screamed, interrupting his mother.

"Nope, you're both wrong. I'm the one who doesn't understand. So explain it, somebody."

Myra moved into the great room and collapsed on the end of the nearest sofa. "I was able to get him out on bail, but with the condition that he wears an ankle monitor around the clock."

"It's not just the ankle bracelet," Russell moaned in disgust, as he moved in front of his mother. "I can't leave this place between six o'clock at night and six the next morning, unless I'm in school or Mommie-dearest is with me."

"What's wrong with that?" Laurell asked.

"What's wrong with it is that I don't intend to be in prison, and no jerk of a judge is gonna tell me what I can do or when I can do it."

"Oh, Russell," Laurell said, "you just don't get it, do you? You've committed criminal acts here and back in Georgia. But you're still convinced that you're right and everybody else is wrong."

He turned so fast Laurell almost fell from the near impact. "And I don't need a sermon from you, either! I've already had to listen to the police, that two-bit lawyer, and the freaking judge. So don't you start."

"Well, somebody needs to start, because you obviously don't get it. Are you telling me you prefer arrest in a jail cell to house arrest here, where you can sleep in your own bed?"

"You should have seen where she left me last night." He pointed at his mother. "I ain't gonna serve time anywhere. Here or there." He turned toward the stairs. "And to prove it, just as soon as I can get my crap together, I'm outa here."

"You'll have to be back by six o'clock, or you'll be in violation of your bail." Mama had risen from the couch and was headed his way.

"Sorry, Mommie. I told you, I ain't serving no time. I'm leaving."

"But where will you go?"

The smirk on his face made Laurell want to deck him. *He's just begging for somebody to take him down.*

"Don't you worry about me. I'll see you around some time."

"But don't you understand," his mother pleaded. "If you're not here at six o'clock, I'll forfeit every penny I had to pay to get you out. And then when they pick you up, you'll go back to the real jail."

"Not if they can't find me, I won't."

The words finally penetrated, and Laurell asked. "Just how much did you have to pay?"

"It was a cash bond. I had to put up ten thousand dollars."

Ten thousand dollars! And this guy wants to jerk us around? I don't think so.

"We can't afford to lose that kind of money," she told him, as she blocked his way upstairs. "If you think you're gonna cost Mama like that, you've got another think coming."

"Then I guess she'd better alibi for me and tell them we're

together, if they question her."

"You walk out of here, and I'm calling the cops myself. Now you get yourself upstairs and stop being such a jerk."

"You're not the boss…"

"I wouldn't go there if I were you," Laurell said, amazed at how quiet and blunt her words were. "You're not going anywhere if I have to sit on you."

With his displeasure hanging out for one and all to see, the young man stormed the stairs and they were soon rewarded with the slam of his bedroom door.

Laurel turned to her mother. "However did you manage to put up that much bail?"

Myra sat with her head in her hands, and Laurell had to struggle to hear her response.

"Daddy's insurance money. There was no other way. It's what he would have wanted me to do."

Somehow or another, I seriously doubt he would have been too happy about this. But I'll give it the benefit of the doubt. So we can pull money to bail him out of jail, but not to hire some help for me.

The reality was that Russell's attitude and its extreme cost, coming on the heels of all she'd done that day, was finally getting to Laurell. Mama was home and not a minute too soon.

"I need you to put together this afternoon's appetizers," she told the woman, who stood leaned against the newel post, still wearing a shell-shocked expression on her face. "I've done about as much as I can today."

"Darling, I've simply got to lie down for a while." She made to climb the stairs.

"Mama, I mean it. You saddled me with breakfast and lunch with no help. I can't hold out to do anything else."

"Tell you what," her mother said, "you rest for a few minutes, and you and I'll have time to get ready for the guests."

"I'm sorry," she said, resentful that she was even having to stand her ground. "I'm off duty for the rest of the day."

"But Laurell, darling, I'm tired, too. You don't know what I've been through today."

Laurell's tongue assumed a personality of its own. "On the other hand, you should know exactly what I've been through. Like I said, I'm off duty for the rest of the day."

"But who's going to help me?"

That's when Laurell's mouth shifted into overdrive. "Why don't you make Russell help you? He's under house arrest, and he just got a ten thousand dollar payday in advance. I'm out of here."

The last glimpse she had as she stormed out the back door, was of her mother with her mouth hanging open.

Mountain Laurell

Chapter Five

How can she be so dense? And so heartless? Can't she see how unfair she is to me? But more than that, she's setting Russell up to take a big fall. Mama is not going to like having to visit him in prison.

Laurell couldn't decide which grieved her more. Her brother was in a dangerous place and their mother's pampering was only giving him permission to continue to skirt the law. At the same time, she was using Laurell as near slave labor.

It's not that I don't want to do my share. But the problem is, I'm doing so much more and getting no recognition.

Laurell wandered the yard so long, she lost track of time. When she finally returned to the inn, it was after the evening guests should be checking in and enjoying their social hour. She wondered how her mother would receive her. The first clue that things weren't normal was when she entered the kitchen to discover the lights off. There was no sign of any food preparation.

Five-thirty, the clock says. Things should be in full swing, but I don't hear any conversation or other sounds coming from the great room where the guests socialize.

A quick peek around the corner verified that nothing was happening on the main floor. Further investigation revealed what was obviously a hastily-crafted sign posted where it could easily be seen. NO SOCIAL HOUR TODAY – SORRY, it said.

I can't believe this! She canceled rather than put herself in the kitchen. This social time is one of the advertising points of our marketing. What if I'd taken the same attitude about breakfast or lunch today?

Her anger had dissipated while she'd been on her walk, but Laurell could feel the fury rebuilding. She also understood what was happening. In her previous jobs, Myra had delegated responsibility, but she'd never had to step in and actually assume any of that responsibility.

Something tells me I'll be handling breakfast by myself tomorrow. But I absolutely will not do lunch without some help.

All she wanted to do was escape into her bedroom and lock the door on all the insanity that reigned supreme in her household. The hunger pangs in her stomach insisted otherwise. There hadn't been time for lunch. In the end, she went back to the kitchen, confirmed that none of the breakfast breads had been mixed to rise, and knew what she had to do.

When she left the kitchen two hours later, all the bread was made and rising. She'd put the breakfast casserole together, and had cleaned and readied all the fresh fruit.

This is the last of the fruit. Need to order more. I'm sure Mama hasn't even thought about it.

She made a note on the chalk board on the wall by the pantry door, and went back to finishing everything that could be done ahead of time. Before she left the kitchen, she put together a plate of leftovers and poured herself a tall glass of tea with three lemon wedges. She headed upstairs to her room, anxious to have the peace and privacy.

Finally, I get to eat.

Her plans were to pile up in bed with one of the books she'd checked out from the bookmobile on its last pass through Hickory Bend. Reading was a favorite pastime, and one that, as of late, had fallen greatly by the wayside.

The same could be said for my painting. Not only has nothing been done to get me a teacher, I don't even have time to think about painting. What's happening to my life?

Laurell could feel her anger building all over again, and she was loath to let it get the best of her. Just as she was about to close her bedroom door behind her, out of the corner of her eye, she saw her brother heading for the back stairway that came out near the kitchen.

He must be headed to make himself something to eat. I'd bet Mama probably hasn't fed him, either.

She felt a momentary flash of guilt that she hadn't offered to fix him a plate when she made her own. Maybe she should offer him that plate now, and go make a second one for herself. It wouldn't take that long, and it was the nice thing to do. Besides, she knew how the kitchen would look by the time he finished raiding the refrigerator.

Without further debate, she called out, "Russell. Yo!" She started toward him and saw him start at the sound of her voice. He hesitated at the top of the stairs. "If you're going down to make a plate, take mine and I'll go down and get another one."

"I'm not interested in your plate, so don't think you can bribe me in to forgetting how you acted this afternoon." His eyes shot pure hatred her way. "I don't need anything from a sister who thinks I ought to be locked up somewhere."

There went his anger again. Laurell set her plate down on the table next to the stairs, and turned to face her brother. "I didn't say you needed to be locked up. I said you need to change your ways."

"Same thing, as far as I'm concerned." His face assumed an expression that Laurell could only describe as cocky and demeaning. "But you won't have me to push around much longer."

"What do you mean by that?" She fought the impulse to grab her brother by his collar and shove him against the wall, then, for good measure, beat him to a bloody pulp. The light bulb came on. "You're not going to the kitchen for food, are you?" She wagged a finger in his face. "You're about to violate your curfew."

His smile was a leer she didn't recognize. "Give the little girl a prize. You finally wised up, huh?."

Laurell knew if he left and the ankle bracelet ratted him out, which it was supposed to do, the situation would be beyond fixing. He would be in more serious trouble, would be behind bars, and worse yet, Mama would lose her ten thousand dollars. There would be the attorneys' bills.

"Russell, why have you suddenly become so unreasonable? What's this obsession you have with seeing how much legal trouble you can stir up?" Her anger had finally gotten the best of her, and the words struggled to work their way around the lump of fury in her throat. She shoved him toward the wall, causing him to fall into a heap on the floor. "You're not going anywhere. It's almost like you want to spend time in jail."

He scrambled to his feet, his eyes consumed with rage, and shoved at Laurell. "You will not put your hands on me, and you will not tell me I can't leave this house."

She knew she'd done the wrong thing, and that he would leave, unless she could redeem herself.

She held her hands out in a gesture of surrender. "You're right, Russell. I should never have shoved you. That was wrong."

"You better believe it was, and if I wasn't going before, I am now!"

Is he telling the truth? Was he really just on his way to the kitchen? Have I made this situation worse?

"Please don't go," Laurell begged. It was obvious that arguing emotions would do no good. She would have to try a different tact. "If nothing else, don't cost Mama all that money. If you violate your home confinement, she'll never get that money back." She would grovel if that was what it took.

Russell appeared to be considering what she was saying, and Laurell held her breath that she'd gotten through to him. "One third of all that money's mine," he informed her. "I can waste it however I want to."

"You think a third of Dad's money is yours to spend any way you like? I'd like to know how you figure that."

From the smirk on her brother's face, Laurell knew he had one more doozy of an explanation.

"Simple. Like what you said, that was Dad's life insurance money. He had to leave it to Mom, because we're both minors. But there are three of us. By rights, you should get one-third, and Mom gets one-third. That leaves the last one-third for me."

Laurel had to agree that his argument made sense. To a point. But only to a point. "I figure Mama would have a different take on this, don't you think?"

"Doesn't matter what she thinks," he informed her importantly. "Dad would want you and me to have his money. But he's not here, and she'll steal it from both of us if we give her the chance." His body language clearly challenged her to disagree.

"So you think Daddy would agree with what you're doing? Even if he did want you to have part of his life insurance, do you really think he'd approve of wasting it on fines and bail and lawyers?"

"If he cares so much about what happens to me, he should have hung around. If he'd been seeing about his own family instead of taking care of someone else, he'd still be alive." The kaleidoscope of emotions that ran across his face told Laurell just how messed up her brother was.

"If he was still here, we'd still be in Atlanta, and Mom wouldn't have the insane idea of buying this white elephant that brings total strangers into our house every night." He hesitated, then added, "This is our house, Laurell. Such as it is. But it ain't home and it never will be for me."

He considered her with a piercing gaze. "Now I'm about to go meet some of my friends." He pulled himself up and put his face right into her face. "If you so much as look sideways at me, it'll be me putting my hands on you this time." The smirk was back. "And I'll make sure you don't get up off the floor." The grin sent spasms of unease up her spine. "I'm not afraid to hurt you."

He whirled and headed down the stairs. Laurell, totally drained of all starch, collapsed on the top step, and considered what had just happened.

He threatened me. He actually said that he would hurt me. When I shoved him, it was an angry reaction. But he would hurt me deliberately.

The question was, how should she handle this? What was done was done. Perhaps she'd been wrong to confront him, but that hadn't been how it all began. Then, when she realized that something more serious was afoot, it had been like an avalanche gaining speed.

Should she tell their mother? And if she did, would it do any good? Would Mama take seriously what Russell was all about, or would she blame Laurell for inciting the incident? Would she take seriously his threat of violence?

I shouldn't have to make these decisions. Russell has a mother who isn't doing her job.

Unable to arrive at a plan, Laurell finally gave up and returned to her bedroom. The remainder of the evening was spent behind the closed door, but her appetite was gone and the plate of food she'd prepared with such expectations, went untouched. Finally, after much tossing and turning, she fell asleep. When the alarm sounded at five-thirty, it took everything she could muster to roll out and confront the day.

She was counting how many mouths she had to feed, including

her own family, when a troubling question arose. *Did Russell even come home last night?* She knew she'd not heard anything to indicate that he had, but she wasn't willing to do anything to confirm his presence in the house. *He made it very clear last night that I'm not his keeper or his boss.*

She continued to assemble the breakfast ingredients, when the sound of the front doorbell interrupted her count of the eggs she was cracking. A glance at the clock told her that it wasn't even six-thirty. *Who could that possibly be at this hour?* After washing her hands, she headed to the front foyer, as the bell sounded a second time, a little more strident this time. *Whoever it is sure is impatient.*

Through the frosted glass in the top of the door, she could see at least two people standing on the other side. It was way too early for guests, and they'd had a full house the previous evening, so it couldn't be a guest who hadn't yet checked in. Could it be guests who'd gone out early, for a run, perhaps? But guests had their own keys.

Laurell swung the door open to find two uniformed law officers standing on the other side. Her heart went to her throat, and she understood even before they spoke, why they were there.

Russell!

The only thing she was unsure about were the specifics behind their visit. Something told her she wouldn't be in the dark for very long.

"Is Russell Wilson here?" The question was posed by the older of the two officers.

"He lives here," she answered.

"But is he here now? That's what we want to know."

How to answer? How to answer? Finally she said, "I haven't seen him this morning, but then I'm always up several hours ahead of him, making breakfast for our guests."

"Can you check his room and see?"

These officers don't back up.

Finally a clear path of action occurred to her. "Why don't I get my mother and let her answer your questions?"

"That's fine, ma'am. We'll wait right here." He favored her with a deliberate stare and said, "Just so you know, there are two officers by the back door."

Alrighty, then. These guys mean business.

Whatever trouble Russell was in, it must be major this time. The temptation to peek into his room on her way to wake her mother was strong, but Laurell resisted. All she wanted to do was wash her hands of all of it. After all, breakfast preparation had come to a screeching halt. Their guests would be expecting their meal on time, and the presence of armed law enforcement wouldn't go well with breakfast casserole.

Laurell slipped into her mother's bedroom and shook her. "Mama. Mama! Wake up. I need you."

Myra turned away from her in the bed and waved her arm in Laurell's direction. "Gotta sleep a little longer."

"You've got to wake up now. There's a real problem."

"You can handle it," Myra said in a sleepy voice. "You can

handle anything."

Not this I can't.

"There are two cops at the door looking for Russell. You've got to wake up."

Myra turned again and looked at her through bleary eyes. "Cops? But why?"

Mama, even you aren't this dense. It doesn't take a genius to put two and two together in this case.

"They're asking for Russell. They want me to wake him."

"So wake him. They're probably here to verify that the ankle monitor is working properly."

Do I tell her or not?

"Afraid not. Russell left last night about eight o'clock, which was after his curfew. Said he was going to meet some friends. I never heard him come back."

"You let him leave? Have you lost your mind? You just cost me ten thousand dollars!" Her voice sputtered, and she began to pull herself out of the bed "I can't depend on you to do anything right."

The words stung Laurell worse than any physical slap could ever hope to.

"I'll deal with this," Myra said, her words dripping with venom, as she left the room.

That's exactly what I wish you would do. Deal with it! But so far, you haven't.

Laurell made her way by the back staircase to the kitchen, where she had to pick up the pace to make up for lost time. Guests had paid for breakfast, and had a right to expect it to be served on time. Many were on schedules. As she worked, she could hear snatches of conversation from the front hall, but couldn't really make out what was being said.

She'd taken the opportunity to look out the back door and sure enough, two officers were stationed there. This was serious.

The sound of heavy boots climbing the main staircase told her the officers were on their way to Russell's room. The sound of them descending faster, almost immediately, confirmed her earlier suspicion. Her brother's bed was empty. Then the front door slammed shut, and Myra was in the kitchen, wearing a most confused and distressed expression on her face.

Laurell was bursting with curiosity but refrained from asking the obvious questions. Her patience was rewarded when her mother said, "Russell didn't sleep in his bed last night?"

She delivered the message with a distinct question mark in place.

Mama still doesn't get it. Russell is on a path to self-destruction, and the only one who can save him is failing him big time.

Laurell said nothing, but continued her breakfast preparation.

"They say he was part of a group that held up a convenience store last night." She looked at Laurell, and her daughter was surprised to find tears puddling up in her mother's eyes. "He wouldn't do anything like that." She slammed her hand down on the prep island. "I just know he wouldn't. I know my son." Her body language

91

indicated that she was suffering badly. "He wouldn't, would he?"

If what he said to me last night is any indication, he very well could be a part of such a hold-up. His arrogance has him convinced that nothing can touch him.

Knowing that her mother was only looking for the answer that would validate the opinion she already had, Laurell said, "I guess we'll find out."

"They said the GPS on his bracelet put him there. But he wouldn't do anything like that." She continued to prattle on, with every other word a defense of her son who, she staunchly maintained, couldn't possibly have been part of such a crime.

Laurell couldn't handle a confrontation right then. Truth be told, she was out of tolerance for any further confrontations, especially when they concerned her brother.

Myra glanced around the kitchen, but didn't ask if there was anything she could do to help. Instead, she said, "You've got it under control. I'll go back up and get ready for the morning."

She's in denial big time. Instead of getting ready for the day, she needs to be out trying to find Russell before the police get him.

The burden of parenting her parent and having to assume almost total responsibility for the inn weighed heavily on her shoulders. How much more could she handle?

Breakfast was ready on time, but Laurell was feeling the results of the exertion that had made the meal happen. The restless night's sleep and the breakfast prep was taking a toll. True to her promise, Myra had been on hand to socialize with their guests, looking as if she had not one care in the world.

Laurell was straightening the kitchen and getting ready to begin lunch preparation, when the phone rang. Knowing that her mother was still interacting with the last of their guests, she answered on the kitchen extension. The voice that responded to her greeting was the last voice she was expecting to hear.

"Laurell. I gotta talk to Mom. Quick."

"Russell! Where are you?"

"Never mind that," he said, and the snarl in his voice told her his temper was about to blow. "Get Mom," he screamed. "Now!"

Laurell laid down the phone and ran to the front part of the house, where Myra was deep in conversation with a departing guest. She approached the twosome, put her hand on her mother's arm, and said, "I'm sorry to interrupt."

Her mother actually brushed her hand away, as she continued to relate to their guest how her career in hospitality lodging had led her to Oak Hill House B&B. "Just a minute, darling. It's not nice to interrupt."

Excuse me!

"Mama," she said, persisting in her efforts to get her mother's attention. "You need to take this phone call. Immediately." She placed heavy emphasis on the final word, hoping to communicate the urgency.

"Take the name and number, and I'll call them back." She never even looked Laurell's way, but continued to wax on about how much she enjoyed being the innkeeper.

Laurell's patience left the building. "Fine. I'll tell Russell you'll call him back. I just hope he can still get a call by that time."

Myra's head did a quick twirl. "Russell? He's on the phone? Why didn't you say so?"

I heard gossip after Mama resigned from the hotel, that the employees weren't at all sorry to see her go. I'm beginning to understand why.

Laurell finished bidding the guest goodbye and returned to the kitchen, where her mother was deeply engaged in a conversation. From what she could hear, things weren't going the way Myra wanted.

"But son, didn't you understand that you couldn't leave this house after six o'clock unless I was with you? Just because you wanted to go didn't mean you could." Her face was twisting in an expression that Laurell interpreted as both panic and anger. "Russell, listen to me. When you walked out that door last night, you cost me ten thousand dollars." Russell was evidently talking. "No, I can't say you and I were out together all night. Besides, the police were here this morning, shortly after six o'clock. They saw that you weren't here, but I was."

Laurell continued her lunch preparation and found that having something to occupy her hands and her mind was actually a good thing. As long as she concentrated on peeling potatoes and making the roux for the chicken pot pie, she didn't have time to think about what might happen with Russell.

Finally Myra slammed the receiver back into the cradle. "He's lost his mind."

No, he's lost his way, and you're not giving him the direction he needs to survive.

"I've got to go. He's hiding out, afraid to give himself up." Myra ran her fingers through her perfectly-styled hair, making wreck of all the work she'd done earlier. "He says he was with the other boys who held up the store, but that he's innocent. He was just driving the car. He promises he didn't know they were planning to rob that man."

He was driving the car. He doesn't have a car, and more than that, he doesn't have a driver's license.

She decided not to point out those contradictions. Better that someone else deliver that news. Anybody but her. And there was one other pertinent piece of information she didn't share. She knew from study of the law in civics in high school, that just because her brother was seated in the car while the hold-up was happening inside the store, he was considered just as guilty as those who held the gun and took the money. Then there would be the charges of driving without a license and insurance.

"You can handle lunch. Right?" The query from her mother came over Myra's shoulder as she hurried to return upstairs.

"Sure, Mom. I've got it covered."

Would it really matter if I said I couldn't?

Laurell slid the pot pie in the oven and turned her attention to the dessert. A quick check of the pantry revealed that she had ingredients for a cherry cobbler. That would be easy and quick. It wasn't until she heard her mother's car leaving the drive that she realized Myra had left without even saying goodbye.

She couldn't even take time to double-check with me.

This was getting old fast.

By the time the last lunch guest had paid and gone, Laurell collapsed on one of the sofas in the great room. She couldn't keep pushing at this pace, and without realizing it, her eyes closed, and she slipped into a restful sleep. It was the shrilling ring of the telephone that roused her, and so heavy was her rest, it took several seconds to get awake and reorient herself.

"Hello!" she screamed as she grabbed the phone on the registration desk. "Oak Hill House B&B."

"Where were you? Do you realize how many times I let the phone ring?"

Mama!

"Sorry," she said, still too groggy to question the wisdom of telling the truth. "I was so tired after lunch, I'd fallen asleep."

"You fell asleep? With the doors wide open? I don't pay you to sleep on the job."

"You don't pay me anything," Laurell said, unable to catch the words before they left her lips.

"That was cheeky, and I won't tolerate it," Myra stormed back at her. "You have a home and something to eat. Count your blessings."

Can't handle the truth, can you?

"What do you need, Mama?" As she tried to tamp down her impatience, Laurell was thumbing through the rooms reserved for that evening, and saw that only three of the previous night's guests had stayed over, and only two other rooms were reserved. At least preparing for the social hour would be easier.

"I'm going to have to stay here for a while. These police are being totally unreasonable, and I've had to fire Russell's attorney." Laurell heard a sharp intake of breath. "Can you believe it, he tried to tell me I was responsible for Russell being out last night. Then, he refused to demand that they allow me to see my child."

I like that attorney. Only he didn't have a clue who he was up against. Wonder if I could get fired for telling it like it is?

"Fine, Mama. You do whatever you have to do. Now I've got to get started on food for the social hour."

"You'd be ahead of the game if you hadn't taken a nap."

"Yes, you're exactly right. So I'll go now and get started."

It was almost eleven o'clock that night when Laurell heard a car pulling into the drive and around to the back of the inn, where everyone parked. She'd been in her bedroom, reading, and got up and made her way to the window.

Mama!

She studied her mother's body language as the woman climbed out of the car and made her way across the graveled turnaround to the back door. Fatigue clearly had taken possession of her body. Taking the back steps two at a time, Laurell arrived in the kitchen just as the back door opened.

Play this nice. She's exhausted.

"I was starting to get worried about you." She moved to the refrigerator, opened the door, and was peering inside. "Have you eaten anything? Are you hungry?" She shuffled some of the contents, looking for something quick and tasty.

"I'm too tired to eat anything," Myra said. "I just want to go to bed." She looked at her daughter, and Laurell saw the accusation before she heard it. "This thing the police have about jumping on my poor child, when he's not really done anything, is unconscionable."

What is it going to take for this woman to see the truth?

Her mother continued with her tirade. Everything she said echoed Laurell's earlier assessment of the situation. According to the police, Russell was as guilty as the other boys. His lack of a driver's license was another charge, and it had taken the third new attorney to finally wrangle visiting rights with the boy.

"Would you believe, I had to hire and fire two attorneys before the third one finally got me in to see your brother."

But I'm sure she had to pay each one of those lawyers. Especially if she fired them. They probably stuck it to her.

"So how was Russell?"

"Oh, Laurell. He's pathetic. You wouldn't believe how nasty that jail is. And they'd taken his clothes and made him wear a hideous orange jump suit that's about three sizes too big. It's so unfair."

Laurell resisted the urge to point out that if you don't want to do the time, and everything that goes with it, you shouldn't do the crime. "What did he have to say?"

"He's innocent, Laurell. He was just in the wrong place at the wrong time. But they're determined to make him the scapegoat."

Never mind that he violated his home confinement. How

does Mom so conveniently overlook that? If he'd stayed here like he should have, none of this other would be an issue.

"So what comes next?"

"He'll go in front of the judge in the morning. Which is why I've got to get some rest. It'll be morning before I'm ready for it." She picked up her purse she'd dropped on the island, and said, "See you in the morning. I've got to be there by ten o'clock, and I've got to have some rest."

And I've got to be in this kitchen at five-thirty, and I need some rest, too.

Laurell didn't feel good about her lousy attitude that she knew was only getting worse. But this constant ignorance of her needs, and all the work she did as well, was getting old very fast. She double-checked all the morning pre-prep, turned out the kitchen light, locked the door, and made her way upstairs.

She was loading the buffet with the various containers of food the next morning, when her mother came through the kitchen. She was dressed for her trip back to court.

"Smells wonderful in here."

Laurell took her words as a compliment and said, "Thank you." Maybe Mom did have some idea of how much work she did.

"Can you fix me a plate? I don't feel like I got any sleep, and this morning isn't going to be pretty."

She bit back the words that begged for release, served a plate and set it in front of her mother. She knew that Myra wasn't overly fond of sausage, so she went light with only two patties, but ladled up a generous helping of the cheese grits made with two different kinds of cheese and cooked in real chicken broth.

"And a cup of my tea?"

Without answering, she drew a cup of Myra's favorite tea, and handed it to her. There was no response, no sign of any appreciation. Myra ate without conversation, even though Laurell was in and out of the dining room, bringing the serving containers and setting the table. When Myra had finished, she rose from the table, leaving her soiled dishes behind, and said, "I'm going up to brush my teeth and get my purse, and I'm out of here."

Yes, your majesty. Of course, your majesty. Laurell picked up the dishes, straightened the table for the guests who would be descending shortly, and returned to the kitchen.

The morning was busy. Thankfully Laurell didn't have to clean rooms, but someone had to supervise the woman who did. Shortly after ten o'clock, the maid, Phyllis, came to the kitchen where Laurell was working on lunch, to say that her son's daycare had called. He was sick, and she had to go.

Knowing that family had to come first, Laurell had sent the woman on her way, after learning that there were still two rooms that hadn't been touched. She'd left the kitchen to check the night's reservations and after counting on her fingers, saw that if they had no walk-in guests that night, there were just enough rooms to get by.

I'm just going to have to gamble. I guess if someone walks in, I'll just have to go make up a room. Or tell the person to go elsewhere.

She could just hear how her mother would react to turning someone away, but right then, Laurell's hands were full cooking lunch.

It was almost three o'clock when the sound of a vehicle slinging gravel circled the house and went silent beside the back door. A peek out the slit in the curtains revealed that her mother was back. If body language was any indication, Myra Wilson was fit to be tied, as Grandmother Wilson would have phrased it.

I'm guessing things didn't exactly go well in court. Between how angry she looks, and the fact that Russell isn't with her, he's probably not getting out of jail this time.

She continued chopping raw vegetables for the social hour, and braced herself for the volcano blast she was certain would happen. However, when the eruption occurred, it wasn't anything like she'd expected.

The back door was slung open, and it crashed against the wall with a loud bang. The look on her mother's face was pure venomous, and the words that poured from her mouth were frightening. As she spit her accusations, Myra was stalking around the kitchen, looking for all the world like a mad woman.

"How could you, Laurell? Do you have any idea what you've cost me?"

The impact of her mother's words caught her totally off guard. "What are you talking about?" She gripped the edge of the island counter, braced to run, if the situation further deteriorated.

"Don't play innocent with me," her mother charged, bending and putting her finger in Laurell's face. "You've always been jealous of poor Russell, and you set him up to get caught." She continued to walk to and fro, opening cabinet doors and closing them, opening the refrigerator and rambling around inside, before shutting the door.

"Jealous? Set him up?" Laurell moved away. "What are you talking about? I haven't done anything to him."

"That's not what he says."

"Then he's lying. " Again.

"So he didn't tell you that he was leaving, and you just let him go?" When she saw the look of panic that captured her daughter's face, Myra's countenance became almost gleeful. "See, I knew he was telling the truth."

"No!" Laurell came back. "He's lying. Through his teeth. He did tell me he was leaving, and he said one-third of Daddy's life insurance money was his. If he wanted to spend it on fines and lawyers, that was his choice."

"You're the one who's lying. Russell would never say something like that."

"Not only did he tell me that, but he offered to hurt me if I tried to stop him."

"Now I know you're lying." Her face twisted maliciously. "Russell doesn't have a violent bone in his body. And now, because of you, he's probably going to serve some time, and I've already lost what I paid to bail him out."

"That's not my problem. I didn't do anything wrong."

"Oh, yes, you did." Myra stopped her pacing, braced her elbows on the counter, and stared Laurell in the face. "You've had a lousy attitude for quite some time, and I've overlooked it. Thought you'd work your way out of it. And this is the thanks I get."

"I haven't done anything wrong, I tell you." Now it was Laurell who was unable to sit still.

"I've got to recover that money I just threw away. You're too old to still be living at home without paying your keep."

Laurell couldn't believe what she was hearing. She wanted to shake her head like they did in the movies, hoping it would reset her brain.

"Starting today, young lady, you'll be paying room and board." She paused, and Laurell could see the calculator keys in her brain in operation. "I'd say one hundred twenty-five dollars a week would be adequate. At least to start. It's not right that you live here and not contribute. And you can forget all about those silly art lessons." Laurell watched the veins in her mother's neck grow and discolor. "Like you could ever make a living as an artist," Myra threw out. "Lessons would be a waste of my money!"

But it's not just your money. Daddy put that money aside for me.

"You don't pay me for anything that I do around here. Now, I'm supposed to pay you for the pleasure of working here like an indentured servant?"

"I don't pay children to do their chores."

Chores! She calls all that I do chores. It was all more than she could handle, and Laurell did the only thing she knew to do.

"You're right. I shouldn't live here unless I contribute. So I'm leaving. You can do everything I've been doing, and we'll see how long you last."

The anger shot through Myra's body, and Laurell fully expected to see her mother's head erupt in flames.

"You're not going to talk to me like that."

"Sorry, I just did. But don't worry. It won't happen again." She put her hand on the back door knob.

"What are you doing? You aren't leaving? I forbid it. You don't even have the social hour foods ready."

"Sorry, Mama. I'm gone. Guess you'll have to finish the finger foods."

By the time she was out the door, Laurell's emotions had seized control, and she stumbled across the back yard, toward the woods, with tears so heavy she couldn't see where she was going.

Chapter Six

Laurell had no clue where she was. When she came back to the world of the living, it was to discover agony worse than anything she had ever known. The only thing she knew for certain was that her entire right leg was engulfed with burning pain. What's more, she hadn't the first clue what'd happened. Or how she'd got there. Wherever it was, she was in a thick forest, because the numerous tree tops blocked out many of the stars and much of the moon. She could barely make out shadowy, twisting trunks clustered around her on the steeply sloping hillside.

All she could say with any certainty was that she was laying sprawled on the ground, on her back. Movement was excruciating, and stole the very breath from her chest. Getting on her feet would be impossible, and it was so dark, she couldn't even see her leg that was hurting so badly. Where was a flashlight when she needed one?

A flashlight! When did it get dark? What time is it?

As she reached for the watch that wasn't on her left arm, where it should have been, finally her memory began to return. Her watch was on the kitchen window sill at the inn, where she'd placed it when she washed the lunch dishes. The last memory she had was of leaving the chaos that her mother and brother had brought to Oak Hill House.

After preparing both breakfast and lunch, and cleaning up

afterward without any help, Mama expected me to help make the afternoon appetizers. She has put Russell ahead of me for the last time. She blames me because he violated his home confinement. It had been the last straw.

But knowing where she had been was little consolation. Where was she now? And how did she get there? How she was going to save herself?

Merely moving even a little caused knife-sharp spasms to shoot through her leg, and she knew it was severely injured. No way would she ever be able to stand on her own.

How long will it take somebody to find me? I don't have a clue where I am, so how will Mama know? Will she even care to know?

The prospect of lying there, trapped, for who knew how long was a sobering thing to consider. More than that, it was scary.

I'm going to die. Right here on the ground, I'm going to die, and there's nothing I can do about it.

Knowing her future and accepting it, she discovered, were two different matters entirely.

As she lay trying to twist into a more comfortable position, Laurel felt tears on her face and realized she was crying. She also finally understood that her injured leg was stuck in a hole up almost to her knee. There would be no getting up on her own. She needed help, and even then getting her leg out of the hole promised to be an excruciating experience.

I guess this is the place where I should be praying. But we've never been religious. I believe in God, but I've never given Him much thought.

The Wilson family had been four people going in four different directions, she recalled, as she lay there, feeling dampness from the ground beneath her seeping through her clothes. Mama always had weekend responsibilities at the hotel. Daddy had been an accountant, who almost always had to work at least part of every weekend, and after-hours many nights.

There just hadn't ever been time for God. She and Russell had no one to drive them, and when the four of them all had a free weekend at the same time, they'd spent it as a family. None of them had wanted to waste half of their rare free Sunday cooped up in a church.

"So, God. Does that mean that when I need You now, that I'm out of luck?" There wasn't an answer to her query, and Laurell quietly told herself that God only took care of those people who took care of Him. Which left her out.

The tears increased, but for a change, she didn't care. If it made her feel better, then she'd just cry. After all, she was going to die all alone. It was a scary thought, but one that she realized was probably going to happen. The situation being what it was, she could lay there for days before anyone found her. No one knew where to look.

I've always wondered if Daddy knew he was dying? Or did it happen so quickly, it was over with before he realized it? At least if I die right here, I'll get to see him again.

She lay there, surrounded by the darkness that seemed to become more pronounced with every minute that passed, and she could hear something running through the woods. Not knowing what kind of animal it was ramped up the fright she was experiencing.

Oh, God, please don't let it be a bear!

She'd read stories about how bears could maul people, and she knew there were bears in the area. In the year they'd been in Hickory Bend, she'd seen the big lumbering creatures more than once. But a cougar wouldn't be good either. Laurell wasn't certain what other kinds of wildlife called the forest home, but she wasn't anxious to meet up with any of them.

The noise was getting closer. And closer. Laurell put her arms across her face, as much to block out sight of whatever was about to accost her, as to protect her eyes.

Then it was upon her, licking her face and whining.

A dog. It's a dog!

While she'd never been a dog person, at least this dog didn't seem to be vicious. Certainly a dog was better than some wild animal that might have killed her. It seemed the worse she'd suffer with this dog was a very wet face.

"Matilda! Where are you, girl?" The woman's voice came out of nowhere, and appeared to originate from an area over Laurell's shoulder. Because of the way in which she'd fallen, turning her head to look in that direction was impossible. But it did appear that a human was connected to this dog that was about to smother her in love.

"You come back to me, girl. It's too dark to be running around in these woods."

The voice appeared to be coming closer, and Laurell took comfort in that. Finally, it occurred to her that she could make her presence known as well.

"Help," she yelled as loudly as she could. "Over here, I'm hurt."

There was no response. Meanwhile Matilda had begun to bark, and dashed back through the thick woods.

"Help me, please," she called out again, suddenly feeling very much alone. Surely whoever this person was wouldn't ignore calls. She yelled again, "I'm hurt and I need you. Please come over here."

When she'd almost given up, the dog came crashing back through the woods, and following closely on her heels was a woman.

"Oh, my," the woman said, as she surveyed Laurell and her predicament. "You've really hurt yourself. Do you think you can walk?"

Laurell had been asking herself that same question, and said, "I can't even get my leg out of this hole. But I doubt if I can walk. It hurts too bad."

While she was talking, her rescuer had walked around to where Laurell's leg was and bent down and shined the flashlight she was carrying for a closer look. "I'd say it's broken for sure. But we're going to have to get you out of there." She reached down and patted the head of the dog that had remained at her heels. "You stay here, Matilda." The dog sat down on her haunches. "Good girl. Stay and take care of this young lady, and I'll be back shortly."

Having been given her instructions, the dog immediately lay

down next to Laurell, where she could easily lick Laurell's face. There was nothing she wanted more right at that moment, Laurell realized, than the dog's attention. If the dog left, she'd be all alone again.

"Where're you going?" she asked. The pain was beginning to really consume her, and Laurell could feel herself getting woozy. "Please don't leave me."

"You'll be okay," the woman said. "Matilda will watch out for you, and I'll be back in just a few minutes with someone to help us get you up."

The knowledge that something would be done comforted her, and before long she could feel herself drifting in and out of consciousness. She had no way of knowing how long it had been, when the dog rose from where she'd been laying and began to bark. Within minutes, the woman, accompanied by two men, was standing over her.

"You came back," she whispered. "Thank you."

"I told you I would. Now let's get you out of that hole."

The woman shined the light again on Laurell's leg, as the two men debated the best way to free her. Finally, with a game plan in place, they began the process. If she thought the pain had been bad before when she was just lying there, it ramped up several times as they began to twist and turn her to get the leg free. Laurell gritted her teeth, struggling to keep the pain from overwhelming her.

"Scream if you want to, honey," the woman said, as she held the light so the men could see what they were doing, which put her in the shadows, where Laurell couldn't see her face. "If it helps to scream, cut loose."

But Laurell didn't want to scream. At that moment, all she wanted was to be back at the inn, in her room, in her bed. Through all the pain had come sudden recall that was equally distressing, of the minutes leading up to her stormy departure. Then, as the men began to try to straighten her leg, it was all too much.

The next thing Laurell knew, she was in a bed, but it wasn't her bed. And it wasn't her room, and the pain in her leg was much worse than it had been. Her entire body ached with a fierceness that threatened to drown her. Only the curiosity of where she was kept her mind off how badly she hurt. There were log walls around her, but it wasn't anything she'd ever seen before.

"Oh," said a woman's voice that Laurell recognized as belonging to her rescuer. "You're awake. Are you hurting bad?"

Unable to speak, Laurell simply nodded her head. She struggled to get a look at the person belonging to the voice that was so comforting and reassuring.

"Here I am, hon," the voice said, as a woman stooped of shoulder, wrinkled in the face, and with gray hair the consistency of steel wool stepped into view. "We're getting help for you. Just try to hang on."

She's the woman from the mercantile! What did he say her name was?

Her leg was hurting so badly, Laurell struggled even to stay conscious, to heed the words of her rescuing angel. Thinking was another matter entirely.

Mary Elizabeth MacCallum. That's her name. But why is she here?

"Are you thirsty?" the kindly voice asked. "Would you like some cool water?"

Laurell shook her head. All she wanted was for the pain to go away.

"Are you sure? You don't want to get dehydrated. It's probably been a while since you had any liquids."

She shook her head again, but the mention of time caused her to wonder how long it had been since she'd had anything to drink. She didn't even have any idea of the time, but figured that it had to be late.

From the other room, the sound of Matilda barking was quickly replaced by the sound of furniture being moved and then, in the doorway, were two uniformed medics pushing a gurney. They wasted little time checking her over. While one applied a blood pressure cuff and got an IV started, the other was feeling of her leg. More than once, Laurell couldn't quell the scream that departed her lips. The pain was overwhelming.

"We need to get you to the hospital," said the technician who'd begun the IV. "You're already in shock, and we don't want it to get worse. We'll be as gentle as we can moving you, but it's gonna hurt. Just to give you a heads-up."

Laurell knew when they started using the sheet she was laying on to slide her over to the gurney. Then the next thing she knew, a bright overhead light was blinding her, and the cloying smell of alcohol and antiseptic assaulted her nostrils. She also knew that her leg felt very strange and heavy. At least she wasn't hurting as badly.

She struggled to speak, to ask questions, but the extreme

feeling of fur in her mouth retarded the words. It took several tries before she was finally able to ask, "Where am I?"

"Miss Wilson," a man in a white coat said. "We're glad to see you awake. How are you feeling?"

"My leg," she said, ignoring his question. "What about my leg?"

"We fixed your leg, but I need to tell you, you really did a number on it."

I've been here long enough to have surgery? My gosh, what time is it? What day is it?"

"Broken fibula, broken ankle, damaged knee cap, and many pulled ligaments. Your recovery time is going to be a while."

"Where am I?"

"You're at Mission Hospital in Asheville. They brought you here because of our excellent orthopedics department."

I'm in the hospital. But I'm supposed to be at home. I just went out for a walk… well, it was an angry walk. But I had to get away.

Reality hit. *I'm supposed to be at the inn. How is Mama operating without me?* The thought of her mother triggered other memories.

"I need to go home," she said, although just the act of speaking was exhausting. "They need me."

"They'll just have to need you for a while longer, because it's going to be weeks before you'll even be able to put weight on that foot."

She glanced around, noting the array of equipment on the walls, and the sterile nature of everything. Of all the places, this was the last place she wanted to be.

"But I have to help at the inn. My mother depends on me." It was one thing to fight being taken advantage of, but it was another thing be sidelined, where she couldn't work when she wanted to.

But do I have a home to go back to? I walked out on Mama and told her handle it herself. She doesn't forget or forgive easily. Do I even want to go back?

The doctor patted her hand. "If you can't do it sitting down, it's not going to happen," he said, not unkindly. "But your mother is right outside. Would you like to see her?"

Oh, no. I never dreamed she was here. Do I want to see her?

There was a part of her that dreaded having to deal with her mother. There was no way to know how she was reacting. More important to her at that moment was understanding what had happened. And how she'd found her way to the hospital in Asheville? Most of all, she wanted to know how the woman she'd frightened at the mercantile had ended up being her rescuer.

Misinterpreting her silence as permission, the doctor opened the door. "Mrs. Wilson, your daughter is awake now."

Laurell couldn't decide how to interpret the expression on her mother's face.

Myra bent over the bed, picked up her daughter's hand, and said, "How're you feeling? Do you need anything?" Her words

116

sounded concerned, but Laurell questioned their authenticity.

You don't have any idea what all I need. Will it do any good to tell you?

But she didn't verbalize what was truly on her mind. Instead, she said, "I just need some sleep, and for my leg to stop hurting."

And I want to know how everything happened! There's so much I don't understand.

"Then you just go to sleep darling. I think they're going to move you to a regular room very soon."

"Mama? Who's at the inn? And what time is it?"

Myra looked at the clock on the wall behind Laurell's head. "It's almost nine-thirty."

"Nine-thirty. Nine thirty at night?" She wished there was a window so that she could see outdoors.

"No, dear. It's nine-thirty in the morning. You were brought in here about midnight, and had surgery about three o'clock."

She processed what she'd heard. "So what day is this?"

"Thursday. Why?"

"Just feel so confused. Don't understand what happened."

"You stormed out on me, and somehow got yourself lost in the woods. You stepped into a deep hole, and broke your leg in several places." The information was delivered in a very dry, matter-of-fact manner that wasn't lost on Laurell. Her mother was play acting again. She could sense the violent emotions below the surface, but knew she was the only one who could.

Boy, that boils it down all right. She's so angry. Whenever she talks quiet like that, she's livid. I'm betting she wouldn't treat Russell this way.

Laurell did some calculations. If it was now truly the next morning, there had been the social hour appetizers yesterday and breakfast this morning that she hadn't been there to even help prepare. And Mama had evidently been here at the hospital. So who was running the B&B? Who was doing the cooking?

"Mama?"

"Hmmmm?"

"You never did tell me. Who's running the inn?"

Laurell could see how her question irritated her mother. The body language was very clear. ""We're closed for the time being. I couldn't be here and there." She gave a huge sigh and said, "Didn't have any choice. Had to send the guests on their way this morning without breakfast."

The long-range cost of disappointing the guests was still to be seen. The financial cost of losing what the industry called bed-nights, and then the loss of today's lunch trade would be substantial. Almost as if Myra was reading her daughter's mind, she said, "None of this would have happened if you hadn't gotten into a snit and stormed out. All I asked was that you help me, and you came unglued."

The woman's hand found the tops of her hips, and she paced the small room. "I hope you're satisfied, because I don't have the money to pay these medical bills. This didn't have to happen, you know."

I knew I'd get the blame for all of this. She still doesn't understand that she has made me basically a… an indentured servant. We learned about that in school. And she doesn't have money to pay my hospital bills, but she can spring for a lawyer and bail for Russell, and not think twice. She's not blaming him.

Suddenly the thought of her mother haunting her in the hospital, resenting every day she was there that cost them business, was more than Laurell could tolerate. All she wanted right then was for her mother to get as far away as possible.

"You need to get back. There's no need to lose business because you're here. There's nothing you can do that the nurses can't handle just as well."

Laurell thought she saw a small spark of relief in her mother's stance, but whatever it was they were giving her for pain, was also beginning to compromise her judgment.

Whenever I was sick and home from school as a child, she never stayed home. It was always Grandma who came to keep me.

"Well, if you really feel that way…" her mother's words trailed off. Then almost as quickly, she said, "I can talk with the doctor before I leave, and you've got a phone." She pointed at the bedside cordless. "You can call me and I can call you." She began to pace again, then stopped just as quickly, and said, "Yes. This might work. Then I can reopen, because we have sold-out reservations for the next three nights."

You aren't thinking that you're going to have to do all the cooking. But I'm too weary to remind you.

"Go on, then," Laurell said and hoped she didn't have to twist her mother's arm. "If you get on the road now, you'll get there in time to greet your guests this evening." She shifted in the bed, trying to find a comfortable position, something that would make her leg feel less like it weighed a ton all by itself. She yawned, and barely heard her mother say, "I'm gone. When you're well enough to leave the hospital, I'll be back to get you."

When she next opened her eyes and looked around, Laurell realized she was in a different room. Whereas everything in the other room had been white on white on white, the walls in this room were an upbeat seafoam green, with coral and yellow accents. She wondered how long she'd been there and again, what time it was.

As she turned in the bed, taking in her new surroundings, she realized two things. The first was that her leg was in a massive cast, encased by wide canvas straps, hanging from a post at the end of the bed. But at least it didn't hurt like it had earlier. The other thing she understood was that very near her right hand was something that looked like a gigantic TV remote. As she studied it, she found a large button with the picture of a nurse on it. She pushed it, and to be sure, pushed it again.

In just a couple of minutes, the door opened and a young nurse with long, dark hair and wearing bright pink, entered. "Oh, you've come back to the real world," she said, and rewarded Laurell with a broad grin. "We've had a pool going at the nurses' station on how long you'd sleep."

"So how well did you do?"

As she spoke, the nurse was checking monitors and the IV line running into Laurell's left hand. "Everything looks good," she said, "what can we do for you?"

The sound of a growl from her gut interrupted the conversation, and Laurell blushed in embarrassment. "I'm sorry."

The nurse waved her hand in an unconcerned manner. "Don't sweat it. Sounds to me like you might be hungry. When was the last time you ate?"

"What time is it?"

She checked her watch and the nurse said, "Four-forty-seven."

Mama had said it was Thursday. "Is it still Thursday? I'm so confused about what day it is."

"It's Thursday."

The information caused her to have to calculate, and even she was surprised when she had to answer, "I haven't had anything to eat since breakfast yesterday morning." She'd been so busy with lunch preparation and clean-up, she hadn't had a chance to eat anything. When she left after the blow-up with her mother, she hadn't been there for dinner.

"No wonder you're hungry. Let me see what we can get for you." The nurse turned toward the door, then spun around with a mischievous grin playing around her lips. "Now, don't you go anywhere."

"Then you better hurry with something to eat, or I'm going out for Chinese."

During the days that followed, the hardest thing for Laurell to accept was that she was a virtual prisoner in her bed. As long as her leg was suspended in the air, she wasn't going to be able to even move around. And every day became a boring clone of the day before. But the doctors told her she was making progress. They were pleased with how her leg was healing. And they promised that soon, although they weren't sure exactly how soon, she would begin therapy and would be able to be more mobile.

I never thought I'd be held prisoner by a bed. If I ever get home, I may never sleep in my own bed again.

Chapter Seven

Every time she thought of home, a siege of unexpected homesickness struck. Despite her many promises, Mama had only called twice in twelve days. Most of their one-sided conversations had centered around her complaints about the work load, and how tired she was. She hadn't one time asked how Laurell was. On the few occasions when Laurell had called the inn, at a time when she knew her mother should have been free to talk, it was never a convenient time.

Day fourteen in the hospital was a memorable day in many different ways, some of them good, and some not so much. It all began when the doctor made his morning rounds. He informed her that her mother was on her way to the hospital, so that they could all talk.

"By this time next week," he'd explained, "you're going to be well enough to leave the hospital."

That sounded like music to her ears. The room was tastefully decorated, but Laurel had grown very tired of what had become a pretty but virtual jail cell.

"So I can finally go home." It would be so good to see the B&B again. That is, if she was welcome there. Suddenly the prospect of being turned away squeezed her heart and brought tears to her eyes.

Only I'll have to pay room and board if I go back. She'll probably expect me to pay this hospital bill as well. The prospect of being homeless caused her heart to ache in ways it hadn't since she'd learned her daddy was dead.

She caught a glimpse of the flash of sadness that crossed the doctor's face.

"Not home, exactly," he said gently, and Laurell sensed there was something he was hesitant to say.

Well where else would I have to go? I have to go home. Don't I?

"You're going to have to have several weeks of physical therapy. The question we have to address is how practical it will be for you to get that therapy at home." He patted her hand. "That's why I asked your mother to come in."

He asked her to come? I'll bet she's peeved.

Indeed, her mother had come, although Laurell confirmed that her earlier assessment had been spot on. It was obvious to her that Myra had better things to do. Less than thirty minutes after she arrived, despite having driven almost three hours to reach the hospital, she was on her way back to Hickory Bend, leaving in her wake one devastated Laurell.

I knew Mama could be unfeeling, but now I'm wondering if she loves me.

When the doctor had explained what would be necessary for Laurell to receive the therapy that would enable her to walk again, in the blink of an eye, Myra Wilson had poured cold water on everything.

"I run a lodging business out of our home," she'd told the doctor. "I can't have a rehab operation getting in the way."

When the doctor had indicated a stair-lift would be needed, so that Laurell could get up and down from her bedroom, Myra had been most definite.

"There's no money for something like that. Plus, it would look bad to the guests."

In the end, Myra left the hospital with no arrangements made, leaving Laurell to wonder if she would be ejected from the hospital to live as a street person.

Mama didn't even ask the doctor what would happen to me if she didn't take me back to the inn. Fat lot she cares. She doesn't intend to forgive me for walking out.

The doctor had picked up on her depression, and when he came back a few minutes later, he said, "We're checking into rehab hospitals, where we can transfer you. There are a couple very close to Hickory Bend, and we're trying those first."

"Oh, that would be great," she told him, allowing her hopes to rise, only to have them dashed again.

"If they have a bed available, we'll try to get one for you. But there's usually a waiting list." He patted her hand again. "Don't let it get you down." He didn't say it, but Laurell clearly heard through what he didn't say that they would take care of her, even if her mother didn't.

Later in the morning, when her nurse came in to check, she

shared that so far, they hadn't found a place that could take her. "But he'll find something. You can count on it," she said.

Laurell had her doubts.

She picked at her lunch when they brought it. It was hard to have an appetite when you were about to be homeless. *I'd love to just cry about all of this, but what good would it do?*

Her spirits continued to lag, and even she was impressed with the magnitude of the private pity party she was throwing for herself. In the midst of the festivities, a knock came at the door. It opened to reveal a small woman dressed in jeans and a plaid shirt. Obviously she wasn't a nurse. It took a moment for Laurell to realize her visitor's identity.

Mary Elizabeth MacCallum!

"It's you," she cried. "I can't believe you're here."

Laurell was still waiting for an explanation of everything that had happened to land her in the hospital. She'd asked questions, and had gotten some answers. Most of which only spawned more questions. *Maybe she can tell me...*

"Girl," her visitor said, "you definitely look a lot better than the last time I saw you."

While she could remember snatches of what had gone down on the mountain that night, the memory of the woman's face over her, comforting her, was the clearest recall she had.

"And you look as welcome as you did that night you found me."

Laurell saw a shudder wash across the older lady's body. "You were in a bad way. I don't even want to think what might have happened if Matilda hadn't sniffed you out."

It was like another piece of the jigsaw puzzle falling into place. *The dog! I remember now. She was licking my face and wouldn't quit.*

"So your dog's name is Matilda?"

"It is. She's a love."

"I'm thankful to both you and Matilda for rescuing me. There's a lot that happened that I still don't remember or understand."

Laurell realized her guest was still standing. "Pardon my manners," she said, and pointed to what she'd been told was the most comfortable chair in the room. "Please sit down, and let's visit. I still can't believe you came all the way from Hickory Bend to see me."

The woman dropped into the chair, situated herself, and said, "I've been worried about you, and finally found out that you were with the folks at the Justice Place." She leveled a steady gaze on the young woman in the bed. "Caught up with your mama yesterday to ask about you, and she didn't seem to know much. Except that your absence was really inconvenient for her and the B&B."

She hesitated, almost as if she expected Laurell to respond, and when she didn't, Mrs. MacCallum went on, "So I decided if I was going to know anything, I'd have to come see for myself."

Am I supposed to defend Mama? I don't doubt that she told this woman that I was making things difficult.

In the end, she elected to say nothing. But her mind was

working overtime, juggling all of her mother's words and actions.

"So what all would you like to know?"

Not wanting to waste an opportunity, Laurell began to pepper her visitor with all the mysteries that had plagued her since she'd come out of the fog caused by all the pain medication.

"Whew," the woman said, "you are full of questions." The smile on her face, however, told Laurell she was more than willing to provide what answers she could.

By the time Mrs. MacCallum left almost an hour later, Laurell had answers and explanations to all her questions, and had learned a lot more besides.

The only part of the day that was still fuzzy was between the time she'd left the inn, angry and determined to go as far away as she could, and when she found herself in such pain. The lure of the receding mountain ranges had beckoned, and she'd made for one of the many trails that led in and out of the forest. Laurell remembered enjoying the quiet and the peace of the woods, the beautiful patterns created by the sun shining through the tree canopy, and the sounds of the summer insects and woodland life.

Beyond that, she remembered nothing, until she came back to consciousness, at some time after it had gotten dark. Her leg had been in a hole, hurting worse than anything she'd ever known.

"I was on my way home from church," Mrs. MacCallum recalled. "It isn't far and I often walk. Matilda was running around with me, and suddenly she struck off through the woods. I called to her, but she wouldn't come back. Which was unusual for her, so I figured there must be something she'd alerted on."

She'd gone on to explain that once she saw how severely Laurell was hurt, she knew they had to have help. "I went back to get the preacher, and there was another member who hadn't left."

Another memory surfaced, and Laurell shuddered, as she remembered the agony of getting her leg free. "They were the two men who got me out of the hole."

"They are. And they also carried you to my cabin. You weren't more than a quarter of a mile from where I live."

The log cabin!

"You live in a log cabin."

"I do," she confirmed. "Been there for better than thirty years. Wouldn't live anywhere else."

"I liked your cabin. What little I can remember of it."

"You'll have to come back to visit me once you get home, when you're up and around again."

She must have noticed the light go out of Laurell's eyes, and the sadness that flooded her face. "Did I say something wrong?" She rose and moved to the bed, where she lifted Laurell's chin and touched the tears that were tracking the young woman's cheeks. "I did say something I shouldn't. I'm so sorry."

By this point, the sobs were in full mode, and Laurell was lashing herself with a mental cat-o-nine tails for allowing her emotions to take her hostage. "It's… it's nothing. Nothing you did." At the look of doubt on her new friend's face, she said, "I promise. It's not you." The next words she wanted to say stuck in her throat, and finally forced their way out around a sob. "It's totally me. I can't go home and get therapy there."

"Can't go home? Why ever not?"

Laurell couldn't bring herself to trash her mother, even though the knowledge that Mama wasn't willing to do whatever it took to bring her home was especially painful.

"It just won't work. The inn is a business and it's not set up to be a rehab hospital." She had decided she'd just borrow her mother's words. They sounded so much nicer than the truth.

"Hrumph," her guest said. "I guess you are bummed out."

They visited for a few more minutes, before the older woman said she would have to leave if she was to get home before dark.

I don't want to see her leave. She's been almost like a lifeline today.

"You hang in there," Mrs. MacCallum advised. "I'll be back to see you." She stuck her thumb up in the air. "Count on me, you hear?"

The remainder of the day seemed long and was definitely lonely. Even a plate of some of her favorite foods was no enticement.

It's good, but I can cook better than this. I miss my own cooking.

But it wasn't just the food. Laurell realized she was yearning for every aspect of her life before the accident. Right at this point, slaving around the clock beat laying up in the bed, unable to get up and move around, and feeling that no one loved you.

No one, except possibly Mrs. MacCallum.

The one thing that Laurell hadn't asked her visitor was why she'd reacted as if Laurell frightened her in the mercantile that day.

I just didn't feel comfortable asking that question. Obviously she's not frightened of me now.

Perhaps, she decided, it had all been her imagination.

Later that night, when the loneliness was more than she could tolerate, Laurell grabbed the phone and dialed the inn. She could tell her mother about the afternoon visitor. *I simply have to hear a friendly voice.*

"Oak Hill House B&B," she heard her mother say. "This is Myra, your innkeeper."

"Mama, you'll never believe…"

"Laurell. Why are you calling? Don't you know the hospital is charging us for any calls you make? I hope you haven't been on that phone all the time you've been there."

"But Mama…"

"Look, Laurell. This isn't a good time. I'm just worn out and need to chill for a little while."

She doesn't want to talk to me.

"You hang up this phone and get some rest, and maybe I can call you tomorrow."

If she's so worried about the money, I could have hung up and she could have called me back. But she didn't think of that.

"Good night, darling. Rest well."

She doesn't even miss me, unless it's in the kitchen.

The hurt that her mother's actions triggered was finally overwhelming. Laurell spent the remainder of the evening crying and remembering, and crying some more. Somewhere in the midst of all those tears, she fell asleep.

"Good morning," her regular day nurse sang out. "Did you rest well?"

Laurell, who'd fallen asleep in the midst of her grief, had trouble casting off the dregs of sleep to get awake. *Oh, my, gosh, I feel like I've been beaten unmercifully.*

"I guess," she said at last, reluctant to confess what a restless night she'd had. As the memories of her conversation with her mother returned to haunt her, Laurell wished she could somehow blot out all the hurt and disappointment.

"Your breakfast will be here shortly," the nurse advised her. "Let's get you awake and ready to eat."

"Why does it matter if I eat? I'm just going to lay here and stare at these same four walls all day."

"Can I come to your pity party?" the nurse asked, as she helped Laurell to sit up. "I love parties."

"It's not a pity party," she said, unable to totally hide the hostility she knew her words contained. "It's a reality party. And the reality is, I'm an invalid and nobody cares about me."

Laurell knew how juvenile her words sounded. She winced at how immature she was acting. But it was obvious that her mother didn't care what happened to her. That hurt.

"I care about you," the nurse said. "You can depend on that." There was a knock at the door. "Ah, there's your breakfast."

"You care for me," Laurel corrected her, as the nurse moved the tray table into position. "You're paid to care for me."

The nurse placed the morning tray on the table and removed the domed cover to reveal French toast and grits and bacon and fresh fruit.

"You're right, I am paid to care for you. But I also care about you, and I don't get paid for that." She unwrapped the silverware and took the top off the coffee mug.

"Now you eat." She softened the harshness of her words with a grin, then added, "And that's an order from someone who cares about you."

Laurell discovered that depression didn't affect her appetite, and French toast was one of her favorite foods.

I guess I'll follow orders.

"Yes, ma'am," she said smartly, as she forked into her first bite of toast, "following orders."

Once she'd finished, her friendly nurse was back to help her bathe and change her gown. They had just finished, when there was a knock at the door.

"Come in," the nurse replied. To Laurell's surprise, the door opened to reveal her visitor from the day before.

"Mrs. MacCallum. You were just here yesterday afternoon."

"And I'm back this morning," the woman said, as she moved

to the chair where she'd sat previously. "I come bearing news."

"News? About what?"

"We'll have to wait for the doctor."

What could she have to do with my doctor? What's going on here?

It was obvious that her visitor didn't intend to share further information, so Laurell gave up for the moment. What else did she have to do to pass the time except wait?

Another knock admitted the doctor, who, she noticed, seemed particularly happy about something. He moved to the bed, took Laurell's wrist and checked her pulse, listened to her chest, and asked her to push and pull against him. Each action was accompanied by a "hmmm."

Finally, he said, "Looking good. Good enough to go home." He retrieved a laptop computer from the shoulder bag that hung at waist level, flipped it open, laid it on her bed, and began to finger the keys.

Going home. Oh how wonderful that sounds. If only it were possible.

"But I can't go home, can I?" she asked. "At least that's what you said yesterday."

"And you still can't go home today. But I think we've come up with something almost as good. Maybe even better."

"You got me a bed in one of the rehab centers near Hickory Bend." It wasn't home, but it was close. At least she'd be near enough to enjoy the mountains she'd come to love.

"Yes. And no," he said, as he returned the computer to its bag. "Neither of the rehabs can take you for at least two weeks, and you need to be there tomorrow, no later than the day after."

"Now you're confusing me," she confessed, and hoped he didn't take offense at the sharp edge on her words.

When you're about to be homeless, it's no fun playing games.

"We've found an alternative location where you can take your rehab, and it's close to where you live."

"Now you've got me totally confused."

"Oh, tell her," Mrs. MacCallum said, intruding into his explanation. "Tell the poor girl she's going home with me."

I'm going to Mrs. MacCallum's house? But how?

Laurell looked to the doctor for confirmation and when he nodded and smiled, she then looked to the older woman, who was positively twitching with excitement.

"It's like this," her visitor said. "I left here yesterday very troubled." Her face echoed her words. "I probably shouldn't talk bad about your mama, but I don't have much use for a woman who won't move heaven and earth to help her child."

Wow! She saw right through Mama.

"So I went to see her when I got back last night." Her face again took on the soured pickle look that Laurell had come to understand meant she was displeased. "I have to say, for someone who was offering to help her like I was, she wasn't very cordial about it." She favored Laurell with a defiant look. "In fact, to be honest about it, she was downright ugly."

Mama, I've always known you had an acid tongue, but honestly…

"But now honey, don't you worry. I'm not holding her behavior against you. But anyway, after I saw how little she cared whether you came home or not, I told her I'd take you to my place. It's all on one level, it'll be a good place for you to recover, and…" she paused and her face lit up in a huge grin, "and unlike your mama, I really want you."

Laurell couldn't believe what she was hearing, and was so fearful she was dreaming, she questioned if she would wake up and discover that she was still a disabled patient with nowhere to go.

The doctor picked up the explanation. "Mrs. MacCallum has graciously agreed to host you for rehab. It'll be several weeks before you're totally ready to begin walking or standing for any length of time without help."

Still afraid to believe her good fortune, Laurell looked from first one to the other.

The doctor said, "You'll be taken by ambulance tomorrow to her cabin in Hickory Bend, and rehab people will come five days a week to work with you."

"It won't be easy," her favorite nurse interjected. "It's going to be painful and tiring. But if you do what they ask of you, you'll be fine."

Laurell knew that some response to her generous benefactor

was required, but the tears that threatened to erupt made talking very difficult. Finally she managed to say, "thank you," and she hoped her eyes and her body language said what she couldn't.

There was one aspect of all this that troubled her, and she knew she'd have to address it to ever have peace. "What about Mama? Is she okay with this?"

The doctor said, "I've talked with…"

"She is," Mrs. MacCallum said, interrupting him. "Especially after I assured her it wasn't going to cost her anything."

Oh, Mama, how could you be so cheap and so crass?

Unfortunately, she had no problem believing her mother's actions.

"But don't you worry, roomie," the older woman said, as she reached to hug Laurell, "I don't hold any of her nonsense against you." She pulled Laurell to her. "We're gonna have a lot of fun. You and me; just wait and see."

The crowd in her room dispersed pretty quickly. The game plan was that Laurell would be carried by non-emergency ambulance the next morning all the way to the little cabin in Hickory Bend, and Mrs. MacCallum would be waiting to receive her. Her therapy would begin the very next day.

"There's no time to lose," the doctor had advised as he talked with her about what to expect. Before she left, Mrs. MacCallum had gotten a list of items from Laurell's room at the inn that she needed or wanted.

"I'll go get all this as soon as I get back to town," the woman had promised. "And I'm not taking any gaff off your mama, either." She hugged Laurell as she made ready to leave. "She needs an attitude adjustment, but we'll save that for another day. See you tomorrow," she said by way of farewell. "I hope you're as excited as I am." She was out the door.

Laurell was surprised to discover that she was excited. True, she was going to stay at the home of a person she barely knew. But whereas when she'd surprised the woman that day at the mercantile and suspected she might be a criminal in hiding, Laurell had no such qualms this day.

Sleep, she'd figured, would be hard to come by that night. "I'm actually excited," she told her nurse. "Bet I'll lie here all night and stare at the ceiling."

That wasn't the case, however. When she next opened her eyes and saw daylight pouring through the spaces in the blinds, she realized she'd slept the entire night through.

"Ready for your big escape?" her favorite day nurse asked, as she came in to prepare Laurell to leave the hospital.

"I am ready, but I've just realized: I'm gonna miss you."

"Miss me all you want," the nurse replied. "But don't grieve." She patted Laurell's hand and began to remove the IV line. "I'll miss you, too. But the fact that you can leave here means I've done my job right."

"Never thought about it like that."

"You just keep that in mind, 'cause I'm counting on seeing you walk back in here on your two good legs someday soon, to tell me thank you."

"And I will," Laurell assured her.

I most certainly will.

JOHN SHIVERS

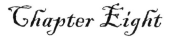

Chapter Eight

The first thing Laurell noticed when she awakened the next morning was that her room was flooded with beautiful light. It was also quickly apparent that the walls weren't anywhere close to the nauseating green that had gotten so ugly and tiresome. She definitely wasn't still in the hospital.

But where was she?

It took a few seconds to realize that she was in Mrs. MacCallum's cabin, deep in the woods outside Hickory Bend. And with that realization, all that had happened since she'd been loaded into the medical transport van at the hospital in Asheville the day before came rushing back to her.

What a time of discovery it had been. Laurell let herself enjoy the memory…

The route through the winding mountain roads carried them through deep verdant valleys with over-leaning peaks and across mountain tops with stunning vistas, until finally the van arrived in Hickory Bend. The driver stopped to consult the written directions he'd been given, and Laurell realized she didn't even know where she was headed.

"How much farther?" she asked the driver, who had begun moving on through town. It had hit her that she had no idea how far

Mrs. MacCallum's cabin was from Oak Hill House, or how far she'd actually walked that fateful day.

We're going to pass the B&B!

"About four driving miles it looks like."

When she realized they were almost at the gateposts to the inn, Laurell had to make the decision of whether to look or not. Her first inclination had been to turn her head to the right and refuse to see her former home. But she couldn't do it, and just when it was almost too late, she'd caved. It was still there, for sure. What hit her hardest was the lack of connection she felt with the place that had been her only refuge for more than a year.

A couple of miles past the bed and breakfast the driver made a left turn onto a narrow strip of country road that wound back into the forest. On the way, Laurell noticed a small building in the edge of an ancient-looking cemetery. The quaint little stone structure with arched stained glass windows and a bell tower caught her artist's eye immediately.

I would love to paint that little church. I wonder if that's where Mrs. MacCallum goes?

She didn't say it, but she'd also wondered what it would be like to go to church.

After the van pulled up in the drive by the little log cabin that looked like it had always been on that spot, the driver and the attendant had rolled her into her new home away from home, where she'd transferred into the hospital bed that was waiting. Then they were gone.

In just the short time she'd been there, Laurell had already spotted several precious personal items that had been in her room at the inn. She wondered how much grief Mrs. MacCallum had endured to get them. That, however, was a question for another day.

The sight of the hospital bed had surprised her, and when asked, her hostess said, "The doctor felt like it would make it easier for you to get in and out of bed, at least for a couple of weeks. He ordered it."

"But who paid for it?" She regarded the woman with suspicion. "Not you, I hope."

"No, no, your insurance paid for it."

"Insurance? I don't have insurance."

"You must have," the older woman said. "Because they paid for this bed, they paid for you to be brought here. They're also going to be paying for the therapy you'll be getting over the next few weeks."

Mama made it sound like she was going to have to pay every penny of my bills out of her pocket. It appears that wasn't exactly accurate. But then Mama seems to have a real problem with truth and accuracy lately.

Once she was settled into her new bed, Laurell realized how weary she was from the long trip. Sleep suddenly felt very attractive.

As if she had read her guest's mind, Mrs. MacCallum said, "I know you'd probably like to rest a while. Would you like anything to eat or drink?"

It was a difficult question to answer. "I'm not really hungry or thirsty, but I want something."

"I've got just the thing."

She returned with a box that had pictures of popsicles on the outside. "How about something sweet and frozen? Cherry, orange, grape, lime, and banana... take your pick."

I can't remember the last time I've had a popsicle.

"I used to love these when I was a kid. But I don't think I've ever had a banana popsicle."

"Banana it is," Mrs. MacCallum said, and with the flourish of a magician, pulled a frozen treat out of the box.

After finishing the banana-flavored ice, Laurell had slept for almost three hours. She awoke with a start, uncomfortable, because she didn't immediately understand where she was.

Then the pieces came together, again, and she realized that she was in a log cabin in the North Carolina woods. As she lay, just taking in her surroundings, one thing registered almost immediately. The walls of the small room were covered in what appeared to be original pieces of artwork.

How did I not see these before?

One thing was obvious. Whoever had painted the many pieces was a very talented artist. Laurell might only have been an amateur painter, but she knew good when she saw it. These pieces were very good.

Oh, how I would love to get out of this bed and get closer to look.

Instead, she vowed to ask about the artist as soon as she could.

In the meantime, she lay back in her bed, as her eyes moved from one painting to another.

"Oh, you're awake." It was Mrs. MacCallum standing in the doorway. "Did that nap help?"

"It did," Laurell said. "Didn't understand how tired I was. It's not like I've been working."

I wasn't this washed out after sixteen-hour days at the B&B.

"Not to worry. You just don't realize you're still weak. Laying in bed day after day will do that to you, so sleep every chance you can, and get your strength back." She moved to the bed and straightened the covers. "Now what can I get for you?"

"You're not going to wait on me hand and foot, are you? I'd feel so guilty. You've already done too much."

Laurell was encouraged by the chuckle that accompanied her hostess's answer. "Well seeing as how you're more or less confined to that bed, what would you suggest?"

While Mrs. MacCallum was trying to soften her response with humor, Laurell knew that beneath her words was a truth that couldn't be avoided. She was trapped in the bed.

"Touché," she said, trying to keep the despair she was feeling from reflecting in her voice. "I wonder if I'll ever be able to walk again. I'm afraid my leg may have forgotten how."

"You'll be back on your feet in no time." She smiled at her patient, and Laurell thought she detected a sparkle in the woman's eye. "I happen to know that you're going to be introduced to a walker tomorrow, when the therapist comes."

"You're serious?"

"The medical supply place brought one when they delivered your bed. The man said the therapist would need the walker for you tomorrow."

The prospect of finally being able to stand up and even try to walk again made her feel that maybe all was not as black as it appeared. Lying in bed all day every day was getting so old.

Mrs. MacCallum had cooked fresh country vegetables for their evening meal, and she brought her plate into Laurell's room, so that they could eat together.

"You've done too much," Laurell protested, as her plate was set before her. "You must have cooked all day."

"Believe me," the woman said, "I don't get to eat this good very often. I love to cook, but it's too much work just for me." She favored Laurell with a big smile. "Thanks to you, I get to eat good for the next few weeks."

"Umm…" Laurell said, unable to keep the moan of satisfaction quiet. "This creamed corn is soooo good. You have to give me your recipe, I could use it back at the…"

As she realized what she was about to say, it occurred to her that she didn't know if she would ever again cook at the Oak Hill House B&B.

"You'll go home again, you know."

How does she know what I'm thinking?

"I don't know if I even want to go back, if I'm still just going to be considered an indentured servant, with no paycheck and no appreciation."

"Your mother will change her attitude as soon as we have a chance to work with her."

We? Where are we getting that?

"I'm going to talk to her, honey. She just doesn't know it yet."

"All she'll do is freeze you out. I've seen her do it before."

"Oh, she'll definitely try. But I've got a pretty thick skin."

They spent the evening visiting, talking, and her hostess read for more than an hour from one of the newest books on the market. Laurell discovered that she and the older woman actually had much in common.

"That's enough for tonight," Mrs. MacCallum said, as the clock hand moved toward nine o'clock. "It's time you took another nap, because tomorrow is going to be a big day." She straightened the covers around Laurell, who for just a moment felt very mothered. "Physical therapy is exhausting, and we want you ready and able."

"Thank you," Laurell said, as she negotiated to find her comfortable spot.

"Sleep well," the older woman said. "I'll see you in the morning. And if you need me during the night, just yell. I'm a very light sleeper."

"I'll be okay. Good night."

Sleep was just about to claim her, when she remembered the question she'd vowed to ask.

How could I have forgotten about all these wonderful paintings? For sure I'll find out tomorrow.

The new day was upon her before Laurell could even get awake good. Following breakfast that was just as tasty as the previous evening's meal, Mrs. MacCallum had helped her to bathe and change into the lightweight sweats the therapist's advance instructions had decreed.

She was barely ready when they heard a vehicle pull into the drive, and very quickly, there was a knock at the door. By the time the pleasant but no-nonsense young man who'd come to help Laurell learn to walk again was gone, the patient understood that therapy wasn't going to be a piece of cake.

"And to think I have to do this every day. Well, except for Saturday and Sunday. I don't think I can do it."

It couldn't have been this hard to learn to walk when I was a toddler. How come this is so much different?

"After tomorrow, it'll be easier." Mrs. MacCallum grinned. "Notice I said easier, not easy."

"How come after tomorrow?"

"Hate to give you the bad news, but because of how hard you worked today, tomorrow you're going to be sore in places you didn't even know you had."

"You're saying I'm out of shape."

Mrs. MacCallum held up her thumb. "You got it. Now, how about something to eat to help you replenish all that starch you used this morning. Then you can take a nap."

"Sounds like a plan," Laurell said, as she relaxed in her bed.

"You want to eat in here or do you want to come to the table?"

The therapist had left specific instructions. She could be on her walker, but be careful to put no weight on the injured leg to go to and from the bathroom, and to come into the living room and the dining room.

"If you don't mind," she said at last, "I'll eat here. But tonight… tonight, I'm going to walk to the table."

"That's probably a good idea. I'll be back shortly with our lunch."

Laurell was actually almost asleep, when she heard the woman's voice she'd come to love.

"Soup's on," the voice advised her. "Wake up and eat."

"Guess I was more exhausted than I realized."

"You worked hard today. I'm proud of you."

Again, she was about to fall asleep, when she realized she still hadn't asked about the paintings. The homemade tomato soup and toasted cheese sandwiches and fresh fruit had hit the spot. Laurell was amazed at how much stronger she felt after eating. But the crowning portion of the meal was the hefty slice of fresh, homemade carrot cake for dessert.

"Did you bake this today?"

"While you were in therapy, I made it for us. I hope you like carrot cake."

"Love it. One of my favorites. There were a couple of times this morning, when I thought I smelled something baking. Wondering what it was sort of kept me going when things got rough."

"Was it that bad?"

Laurell had to study, before she said, "It was bad, and it hurt a good bit, but I guess most of the problem was that I didn't know exactly what to expect."

Her host handed her the plate with the cake. "Then you've more than earned this." She watched, with her joy evident, as her guest forked up the first bite.

"Ummmmm…" Laurell said. "Oh, this is scrumptious." She forked up a second bite and studied it before popping it into her mouth. "You use crushed pineapple in your recipe. I do, too."

The woman nodded her head. "I think it adds to the flavor, but it also helps keep it moist." Her mouth made a grimace. "It's a waste of good ingredients if your cake comes out dry."

For sure this isn't dry!

"Well, enjoy your cake, and then enjoy your nap. This evening, when you come to the dining table, we'll have a virtual celebration."

Still pumped from her morning of learning to use her walker, Laurell found that she suddenly didn't want to waste any more time sleeping. It seemed that was all she'd done for days. The bed was getting really old, and she had the urge to get up and go.

Her body had other ideas, which included a long nap.

The sun was low in the afternoon sky when next her eyes

152

roamed the dark log walls of the little room.

Dr. Walter said I'd probably be here at least six weeks, maybe seven. But since I'm evidently not welcome at the inn, what does it matter? I just don't want to be a burden on Mrs. MacCallum.

It took several minutes before Laurell remembered that she could get out of bed under her own steam. The best game plan, she knew, would be to ask for help until she got better at making the transition to her walker. But she was tired of having to have help. While it took what seemed an eternity, finally she had the walker in position, her hands were braced on it, and she was ready to stand. It was a momentous time.

"Here, here," Mrs. MacCallum's voice said, interrupting the moment of achievement. "Are you strong enough to attempt that by yourself?"

Unwilling to lose the moment of triumph, Laurell said, "You decide. You're here, just watch me and see." She concentrated on the task at hand, and slowly, albeit with a couple of false starts, she stood, shaky at first. Gripping the handholds for fear she'd fall flat on her face if she turned loose, she turned to get the assessment.

"So how does it feel?"

Laurell thought about the question. "It feels great. I'm really tired of laying in the bed all the time." She glanced down at her leg, encased in the new cast the doctor had applied just before she left the hospital. "But I tell you what, I'd never have been able to manage with that old cast. Man, that thing was heavy."

"So are you ready to go to the living room?"

In answer, Laurell put her best foot forward, went to bring up the other foot, and then jerked to a screeching halt before she ever really got started. It had seemed so simple when the therapist was working with her, but going solo was a different story.

Mrs. MacCallum was quickly at her side, steadying the walker. "Don't want you to fall again." She regarded Laurell with a kindly gaze. "Tell you what. You're so tired of the bed, and who wouldn't be. Let me help you to the living room, and you can lie back on the couch and watch TV, while I get our dinner on the table.

It seemed to take an eternity, but finally, Laurell was comfortable on the sofa, TV remote in hand, and was surfing the channels.

I watched more TV in the hospital than I have since we moved to Hickory Bend. That's all there was to do when I was trapped in bed, and there was never time at the inn to enjoy any of my favorite programs.

She was still trying to decide between a rerun of "The Beverly Hillbillies," "Jeopardy," or the early segment of the evening news out of Asheville, when a knock came at the door. Out of habit, she made to get up from the couch to answer it, before she realized it wasn't happening.

Besides, it's not even my house.

"I've got it," Mrs. MacCallum said as she breezed through the room, wiping her hands on the tail of the multi-colored apron fastened around her waist. She pulled the door open, Laurell noticed, without checking to see who was on the other side.

"Well, hello," Laurel heard her say. "Come right on in this house." She stepped aside, and Laurell caught sight of a young man

154

she didn't recognize.

"Hope I've not come at a bad time," the visitor said, as he glimpsed Laurell. "I didn't realize you had company."

"Not a problem," Mrs. MacCallum said. "You remember Laurell, don't you?"

"I do," he said, and smiled at her.

He may remember me, but I've never seen him before. He's good enough looking I wouldn't forget, especially with that naturally curly, golden blond hair.

"You're looking much better than you did the night we pulled you out of that hole. I trust you're also feeling better."

He must have been one of the men who rescued me and brought me here.

Mrs. MacCallum moved to the couch, touched the man's shoulder, invited him to sit in the chair across from the couch, and said, "Laurell, this is Reverend Bill Lowry."

Laurell found herself momentarily incapable of speaking.

'It's good to meet you again, Laurell, but under much better circumstances this time."

"Bill is also my pastor," Mrs. MacCallum said. "I was on my way back from the church that night, and I took a chance that he was still there and could help us."

"George Warren and I were just locking up when this good lady arrived," the young pastor said.

Her tongue finally engaged, Laurell said, "I'm very thankful you were. You two were lifesavers. Literally."

"I must say," he said, "you were in pretty bad shape. Looks like they've got you fixed up."

"She's mending well," Mrs. MacCallum volunteered. "But she's still going to need to be here for several weeks while she takes therapy."

"So you're running a rehab hospital now, are you?"

Laurell could tell from the gleeful look on the man's face that he was having some fun with his church member.

"I never know what to expect from you next."

Evidently this pastor and Mrs. MacCallum were accustomed to joking with each other, because each was totally comfortable.

He's probably the first preacher I ever met. I didn't know they would have a sense of humor.

"Laurell's mother runs the Oak Hill House B&B in Hickory Bend, but she doesn't want Laurell underfoot." Laurell saw sparks fly from the woman's eyes. "Personally, I'm glad for the company."

Mrs. MacCallum doesn't back up from telling it like it is. I hope the preacher doesn't think badly of me.

His words provided immediate reassurance. "You're in good hands here. Mrs. MacCallum is a good friend to many, and I would imagine you're on that long list."

Before she could respond, Mrs. MacCallum said to the minister, "Where you eating tonight? I've got plenty."

Laurell glimpsed but didn't understand the look that passed between the preacher and her host.

"Bill here is single and was about to kill himself with his own cooking," her host said by way of explanation. "Different members have started having him for at least one meal a day." She chuckled and added, "We don't want to lose him, so we feed him."

"And I would be glad to eat with you tonight," the preacher said with no hesitation or shame. "It was going to be a frozen dinner if I was left to my own devices."

Mrs. MacCallum appeared to find his choice for an evening meal very unpalatable. Her face conveyed her distaste. "Then you just sit here and visit with Laurell, and I should have everything on the table in just a few minutes."

What do you say to a preacher? Are you supposed to pray with him or something?

Laurell realized that she had no idea how to act around church people. Mrs. MacCallum was one, and Laurell was going to be a guest for several weeks. Would this get awkward?

"So tell me about yourself, Laurell. You haven't lived in Hickory Bend long, have you?"

Without going into grand detail, she hit the high spots of how her mother had come to move the family to North Carolina.

"It goes without saying," the young minister said, "that I'm sorry for the loss of your dad. It looks like things have worked out for you." He gestured toward her bum leg. "Well, except for that bad leg. And even it could turn out to be a blessing in disguise."

Not very likely, preacher. But I guess that's what he's supposed to say.

As if he didn't really expect an answer, he continued. "So what do you do in your spare time? Do you have hobbies?"

How do I tell this man that I don't have any spare time, never mind time for a hobby?

Finally she said, "I stay pretty busy at the inn, but when I have a few minutes, I love to read."

That launched him on the subject of some new books that had recently been released. Laurell was thankful once again for the bookmobile that traveled into Hickory Bend every two weeks. She was always there when the big, cumbersome truck-looking vehicle pulled up beside the Twin Lakes General Merchandise. Her only regret was that there were more books on those shelves than she would ever have time to read.

The preacher launched into a debate over two current popular authors, and Laurell was relieved to find that she and the minister shared a mutual love for both.

This man seems almost human. He's not at all pious or head in the clouds. Have I got it all wrong?

She remembered barbed comments her mother had made about several preachers in Atlanta, and she'd formed her impression of all pastors based on those observations.

The more I think about all that Mama has shown me, the more I wonder, should I be leery?

She found herself wanting to engage him in further conversa-

158

tion, when Mrs. MacCallum's voice dictated otherwise.

"Dinner's served. You stay right there, Laurell, and let me help you get to the table."

The pastor rose and asked, "Laurell, can I help, or would you rather I stepped back out of the way?"

Before she could answer, Mrs. MacCallum said, "No offense, Bill, but you trip over short nap carpet."

He laughed and said, "Then let me move myself out of the way and I'll leave you two to make this happen.' He winked at Laurell, who'd almost feared he was offended, and said, "You see how she treats me? Absolutely no respect."

There was that hilarious give and take again.

Mrs. MacCallum held the walker steady while Laurell swung around on the couch, put her good foot on the floor, her hands on the grips, and braced herself to pull up into a standing position. It was more exhausting than serious exercise. Literally one foot at a time, she made her way the twenty feet to where the dinner table was set for a meal. The various dishes were most appetizing, and Laurell had to chuckle to herself. Her grandmother had always said everything was always better when you didn't have to cook it yourself. She was suddenly starving, and had a new appreciation for her grandmother's sentiments.

"Bill, will you return thanks," Mrs. MacCallum said. "You always do it so beautifully."

"Let's tell God how appreciative we are," the young minister said.

What am I supposed to do? This doesn't seem like any of the few times I've ever been where a blessing was said. Then it just seemed like something they did. He makes it sound like he's just going to have a conversation with God.

And that was exactly what it was, she was to decide later, in the privacy of her room, under cover of darkness, as she replayed yet again the preacher's words that had blessed their food. But he'd done more than simply say thank you for the meal. He had talked about people in the church who had needs, and had even thanked God for Laurell's recovery, and prayed that He would be with her until she was totally healed and back to life as usual.

As she considered all that the man had said, she realized she couldn't remember one single time in her life when someone had prayed specifically for her. For sure, she'd never thought to pray for anyone else.

I've never really prayed at all. Why do I suddenly feel so guilty?

In fact, something had happened when the young pastor had offered up their blessing. There had been a strange stirring in Laurell's heart, and she had wondered for a moment if it was a side effect of her accident. Finally, she'd decided it wasn't anything to worry about, but neither could she explain it.

Sleep came easily. Laurell realized the next morning, for the first time since the exhaustion she'd known for so long at the inn had first affected her, that she'd slept an untroubled and restful sleep. It felt so good to wake up with energy instead of dread.

After a good breakfast that she enjoyed in bed, the therapist was there. It was another morning of struggle and pain, and the urge to say, "I can't do this…," and then it was over.

Lunch followed, then another long nap, dinner and the enjoyment of sitting with Mrs. MacCallum in the living room, until time for bed again. Every day assumed a similar pattern, although Laurell could tell after several days that her strength was building and the length of her afternoon naps was less. She particularly enjoyed the evenings, when the two women watched TV, read, or just talked.

It had been during one of those times that Laurell had finally remembered to ask the question that had plagued her. "I'm curious," she said, during a lull in the conversation, "all those paintings in my room. Who's the artist? They're so beautiful."

For the first time since she'd known her hostess, Laurell couldn't miss the look of extreme sadness that crossed her face. The ever-present spark that was always in her eyes disappeared, as if a shade had been pulled, and for just an instant, the woman appeared to be a study in grief.

Fearful she'd been out of line, Laurell said, "I'm sorry. It's none of my business."

But like trying to put toothpaste back into the tube, the words she'd spoken so innocently couldn't be taken back. Finally, after what seemed an eternity, the older woman spoke.

"My daughter," she said, in a tone totally different from her usual upbeat but blunt manner. "She was very talented." Laurell realized the answer to her question had been phrased in the past tense.

Her daughter is dead?

Laurell knew better than to probe for more information, although the answers she'd been given had only generated more questions. She would not ask them. As it was, she hoped she hadn't permanently damaged the relationship she'd developed with the older woman.

They were silent for a while, and Laurell realized she was holding her breath.

What do I say? What do I do?

"You must be tired," Mrs. MacCallum said suddenly. "I know I am. Let me help you to bed, and we'll make a fresh start tomorrow."

Laurell didn't resist and soon was in bed, the light was out, but her mind was more active than ever. There was a story behind the paintings, and whatever that story was, it had broken Mrs. MacCallum's heart. Curiosity was overwhelming, but she vowed to ask no further questions. At the same time, she realized that the many pieces of beautiful work that surrounded her were causing her to yearn for a brush in her own hand again.

When morning came, Laurell was conflicted when her hostess entered to help her out of bed. Would the uncomfortable wall that had sprung up between them the previous night still be there? If it was, how would she deal with it? To her relief, Mrs. MacCallum was her usual bubbly, upbeat self, and Laurell breathed a sigh of relief.

I would never do anything to hurt this sweet, sweet woman. But how could I have known that one simple question would unleash that much grief?

There was no reprise of that awkward moment, and while Laurell was relieved, she realized that her curiosity was still building.

162

No good could come of indulging it.

On Saturday, the therapist didn't come, but Mrs. MacCallum had insisted that Laurell continue with her various exercises.

"You'll be without tomorrow for sure, so better we do it ourselves today."

"Why can't we do these exercises tomorrow?" Laurell asked.

They were sitting at the breakfast table, lingering over the last of a loaf of freshly-baked banana bread and fresh fruit. They had been making plans for the day, and Mrs. MacCallum had shared that she had to go grocery shopping sometime that day.

"Since we've been eating regularly around here, the pantry is starting to show many empty spots."

She's been cooking for two. No wonder she has to go shopping. She's caring for me with no compensation. Doing Mama's job.

As if she knew what Laurell was thinking, Mrs. MacCallum said, "And before you go blaming yourself, I don't want to hear any of that. Like I already told you, I go days here and barely eat, because it's no fun cooking and eating for one."

"Still…"

"Still, nothing. You've been a blessing to me and I wouldn't have it any other way. And as to why we can't do therapy tomorrow, I guess we can. Tomorrow afternoon."

"Tomorrow afternoon? What do you have to do in the morning?"

"Why church, of course. We'll be in church in the morning."

At the baffled expression on Laurell's face, the woman said, "Tomorrow's Sunday. You don't go to church?"

Laurell knew her hostess wasn't deliberately being cruel, but at the same time, when she had to confirm Mrs. MacCallum's assessment, she was left feeling almost unclean.

"No ma'am, the only time I've ever been in church was when my grandmother died about five years ago. As it is, I don't remember very much about it."

"Your parents never took you to church? Not even when you were a child?"

Laurell felt about two inches high. "No, ma'am."

"Well then, do you have a problem going with me tomorrow? You already know Bill, and we're a friendly bunch."

Did she have a problem going to church? It would all be new and strange, but as Mrs. MacCallum said, she'd already met the pastor, and he seemed to be a nice guy. She couldn't bear to hurt her hostess's feelings.

"I guess I can go," she said. "I won't know what to do." She remembered a service she'd seen in a movie once, where the congregation had been very spirited and active. "I won't know when to sit and when to stand and… and…"

"We're not fancy like that," her hostess assured her. "Besides, you're going to have to stay seated. She rose and began collecting the dirty dishes. "Let me get the kitchen straightened, and we'll get on with your therapy."

Following a session when Laurell had to confess that Mrs.

MacCallum was more demanding than her regular therapist, they had lunch, and Laurell lay down for her afternoon rest. She'd stopped calling it a nap, because that sounded so juvenile. Mrs. MacCallum had left to drive to Meadeville, where she could shop at a regular supermarket.

"Mr. Holland is good for quick stuff, but he doesn't carry everything I like," she'd said before she left and grinned in the manner that Laurell had come to appreciate. "Plus, I don't like him picking out all my groceries. He deliberately gives me inferior produce, because he can't sell it to anyone else."

That explains why Mr. Holland said he doesn't see her regularly.

Laurell had to stifle a chuckle at the mental picture of the old storekeeper with his glasses perched on the end of his nose, deliberately picking through the potatoes looking for those about to go bad, and bagging them for Mrs. MacCallum. She also couldn't see her hostess standing still for that. Then that earliest memory came flying back into her mind.

Without stopping to debate the merits of her question, she said, "That day I first saw you at the mercantile, did I startle you or frighten you?"

Just as it had been with her previous inquiry, she saw grief overtake the older woman; then just as quickly, it was gone.

"You just startled me," Mrs. MacCallum said at last, although there was no personality in her voice. "You reminded me of someone I hadn't seen in a long time."

Then she'd left for her shopping.

If she hadn't seen that person in a long time, she obviously wasn't glad to see them, either.

Laurell had gotten up from her rest unassisted before Mrs. MaxCallum returned and was on the couch, reading a mystery she'd found among those on the shelves at the end of the living room.

I've got books back at the inn that are overdue to the bookmobile, and I need to get some more to read. I'll ask Mrs. MacCallum how we can do it.

Thoughts about the books and the inn reminded her that in all the time she'd been at Mrs. MacCallum's, her mother hadn't visited. Not even once. She hadn't even called.

She didn't even check to see if I made it from Asheville okay.

Laurell was deep into who found the body, when she heard Mrs. MacCallum's van pull into the turnaround area. In quick order, the back door swung open, and she heard her name being called.

"In here, in the living room," Laurell answered.

Mrs. MacCallum rushed in, waving a newspaper. "Here," she said, momentarily out of breath, "you gotta see this." She thrust the paper toward Laurell, who questioned what was so urgent, even as she grabbed it.

"Front page," the woman said. "Bottom corner."

Laurel looked where she'd been instructed, and the very breath caught in her chest. She wondered momentarily if she was about to pass out and struggled to reorient herself. Then, not believing what she'd just read, she took a second look.

DETENTION INMATE ESCAPES, MANHUNT UNDERWAY

But it was what was beneath the ominous headline that proved most disturbing. Clad in his orange jail clothing, standing against a background of black and white height marks, was the grinning face of Russell Wilson, her brother. The escapee.

Chapter Nine

"It was all over the supermarket," Mrs. MacCallum said. "When I saw the paper, then it all made sense." She laid her hand on Laurell's shoulder. "I knew you'd want to see it."

Laurell went back to the beginning of the article and quickly read through to the end. "Says here that he took advantage of an exercise time in the outside common area and sneaked out through an open gate. They don't think it was a planned escape, but that he saw the opportunity and took it."

He just keeps doing stupid.

"Oh, Mrs. MacCallum," she said. "I'm not excusing what my brother did, but I'm telling you, he's so messed up."

Her heart hurt, but she also knew that it was out of her hands to do anything to turn around this really tragic situation.

I can see now that he's been running wild since Daddy died. Mother was too wrapped up in herself to see that either of us had problems, but Russell's messed up for sure.

"It does appear that way. What's more, from what I heard in town, he's looking at some really serious jail time when they catch him."

Laurell looked back at the headline on the article again, and the words "manhunt underway" caught her eye. "But don't you see," she said, "he's not a man. Not yet, anyway. But he is a terribly confused young man who's lost his direction."

"Did you see the quote from your mother?" The older woman pointed to a portion of the story that was continued on the back page.

"I didn't even realize that wasn't all of the article." She quickly scanned the short section that wrapped up the details. "Oh, no," she said, "listen to this." She began to read aloud.

"Mr. Wilson's mother, Myra Wilson, owner of the Oak Hill House B&B in Hickory Bend, when contacted, said, 'My son is innocent in that robbery. I don't care what the police say. And he should never have been in that horrid jail to begin with. Personally, I'm glad he's out.'"

Laurell felt herself go sick to her stomach, as she re-read her mother's response to the reporter. She had no problem believing that Myra had uttered those very words. Instead, she took them to indicate just how seriously messed up her mother's thinking was, as well.

"Look here, Mrs. MacCallum. The reporter goes on to say that he spoke with the police chief, who said if someone assisted Russell, that person will be in serious trouble as well."

Without saying it, they're implying that Mama may have been his accomplice. None of this can turn out well.

"What am I going to do? What can I do?" She gestured at the walker and then at her leg, and for the first time since she stepped into that hole in the forest, and her entire life turned upside down, Laurell felt the stirrings of overwhelming anger boiling inside her.

"I don't know who to be most angry with, Mama or Russell. Or me?"

"You? How could any of this be your fault?"

Laurell explained the many ways Russell had been in trouble back in Georgia and since arriving in North Carolina. "If only he hadn't left the house that night, none of this would have happened." She felt the weight of guilt overtake her, and said, "I should have stopped him from going to meet his friends."

"Harrumph!"

The sound of disbelief, or was it disgust, that issued from her hostess's mouth caught Laurell by surprise. Before she could question it, Mrs. MacCallum said, "Now you just quit beating up on yourself, my dear. Your brother would have left that night no matter what you did. And why was it your place to keep him from going wrong?"

"But he's my brother."

"And where's your mother in all of this? What's she doing to try and keep him on the straight and narrow, as my daddy used to say?"

Laurell bit her lower lip as she considered the question. How was she supposed to answer without trashing her mother?

In truth, if Mama had made him act like he should a long time ago, many things would probably be different now.

"I know you don't want to talk bad about your mother," Mrs. MacCallum said, "and I don't want you to. But I can say what I think, and I'm not impressed with her style of mothering. For either one of you, for that matter."

171

Mrs. MacCallum is right. Mama refuses to do anything for me and she's done so much for Russell it's ruined his whole life.

The urge to be back at the inn was suddenly more than Laurell's emotions could handle. Whether it was homesickness or worry for her brother, but finally she was so overwhelmed, the tears came. When finally she was able to rein herself in, she found Mrs. MacCallum eyeing her sympathetically. The shame of it all overwhelmed her.

"I'm sorry," she said, while silently pleading for the older woman to understand and accept her apology. "You've been so good to me, I don't want it to look like I don't appreciate it."

"My dear, I know exactly what you're feeling. There's no need to be uncomfortable about your honest emotions. After all, this is your mother and your brother we're talking about."

"I feel like I need to go over to the inn and check on Mama. Regardless of her big talk to that reporter, this has to have hit her hard." Then, lest her words be taken as a hint that she wanted to stay at the inn, she said, "I just want to check on her. Then I'm more than anxious to come back here." Another troubling thought hit her. "That is, if you still want me."

"And why wouldn't I still want you?"

"Because my family is so messed up... so abnormal." She buried her head in her hands. The accumulated insanity that had slowly increased since her father's death finally was too much. Again, she couldn't hold back the waterworks. "I sure wouldn't blame you if you asked me to leave." The knowledge that she couldn't even leave without help only increased her angst.

Mrs. MacCallum said nothing for the longest time. Instead,

she just patted Laurell's shoulder, until finally her guest began to get control of her tears.

"My dear, now you just stop putting yourself down. I could tell you stories of my family that would horrify you, but never would I ask you to leave because of what your family has done."

"But… but I just feel so helpless." Laurell waved her arms in a gesture of frustration and hopelessness. "It just seems like I ought to be doing something to make all of this right." She glanced down at her bum leg and slapped the side of the walker. "As it is, I can't even help myself."

The older woman took a seat on the sofa next to her distraught guest. "Tell you what," she said, finally. "If you'd like, after church tomorrow, we can go to the B&B. Maybe then you'll feel better."

Or maybe I won't. But if I don't go, I'll always wonder. And worry.

The rest of the evening passed quietly. They enjoyed the grilled salmon and green salad that Mrs. MacCallum had made after she'd unloaded the groceries and put everything away. She'd also picked up a German Chocolate cake at the supermarket bakery.

They'd taken a couple of bites of the cake, and each one looked at the other.

"It's not as…," Mrs. MacCallum said.

"…good as it should be," Laurell said. "These are just regular chocolate layers. They cheated and didn't use the right chocolate."

"You sound like you know a lot about cooking." Mrs. MacCallum continued to fork into her dessert, but it was apparent she'd lost interest.

Laurell forked another bite of cake and put in her mouth. "The frosting is the real thing. That's why it looks like a genuine German Chocolate cake until you cut into it." She used her fork to separate a piece of the layer. "Legitimate layers are a paler brown, not dark brown like these layers." She started to eat another bite and put her fork back down. "I wouldn't say I know a lot about cooking. But I knew enough to fix breakfast and lunch and the afternoon social hour foods by myself."

"You're but a slip of a girl," her hostess said, the horror of the situation obvious in her voice. "Do you mean to tell me your mother didn't have someone to help you?" She hesitated. "Surely she helped you herself."

You know, as I look back now, I can see things so differently. In the beginning, Mama claimed that I was helping her. But in truth, I've always done most of the work and she helped me when and how she pleased. Of late, it's been more and more me alone.

"Well, I never…" Mrs. MacCallum's words trailed off. "Let's talk about something else, before I get mad."

Wisely, they did change the subject, and Laurell talked about her dream of becoming an artist, and it was on that note that they closed down the house and retired to bed.

Sunday promised to be a busy day.

It wasn't until after they'd gone to bed and the house was dark and quiet, that Laurell had a chance to reflect upon the evening. She couldn't decide what troubled her more. For certain, the news about Russell was very bad, and Mama was probably going to be in an equally bad way. Especially if she had somehow managed to help the boy escape. Unfortunately, it didn't take much of a stretch of the imagination to suspect that she was indeed involved.

The other part of the evening that bothered Laurell was Mrs. MacCallum's almost non-existent interest in her professed love of art. As she recalled sharing her dreams of being an artist, she realized that the normally bubbly and outspoken woman had been strangely quiet.

Her own daughter was an artist. The walls of this room are covered in pieces of her work. So why wouldn't Mrs. MacCallum have encouraged me, or at least acknowledged what I said.

Yet Laurell wasn't comfortable asking the woman who had been so incredibly kind to her. Her last Q&A had definitely caused upset. She didn't want to make that mistake again.

Despite her curiosity, she slept the night through until the smell of breakfast cooking awakened her. While her appetite wanted her to bounce out of bed, her body had other thoughts. It took a couple of tries before she was able to stand up and stagger, using her walker, to get to the bathroom.

Mrs. MacCallum had made fresh cinnamon rolls and fresh fruit for their breakfast.

"Umm... this is soooo good," Laurell proclaimed, as she popped yet another piece of pastry into her mouth. *It is so nice to have someone to fix breakfast for me.*

"You have to share your recipe with me. I've never tasted such scrumptious rolls." She indulged in another bite. "How do you get the cinnamon flavor so intense?"

"You can have it, of course." Mrs. MacCallum rose from the table and reached for Laurell's plate and glass. "Now we need to get ourselves ready for church."

The delicious food she'd just enjoyed suddenly shifted in her stomach. Either that, or the prospect of attending church had given her a bad case of butterflies.

If only I had some idea of what to expect. The only comparison I have is a funeral, and somehow, I don't think it'll be like that. At least I hope it won't.

Before nerves had time to really do a number on her, Laurell found herself hobbling up the walk to the little chapel where Bill Lowry was the pastor. When he glimpsed her slowly making her way into the center aisle, Laurell saw, his face light up.

"Laurell, it's so good to see you up and out. Welcome to our church this morning." He moved to let Mrs. MacCallum pilot Laurell into a pew. When she was seated, the pastor called out. "George! Look who's here."

A young man seated on the piano bench on the other side of the church looked up, and Laurell saw a sign of recognition on his face. He slid off the bench and made his way to where she was sitting.

"Well, well, you look better than the last time I saw you, I'm happy to say."

Laurell added two and two, concluding that he was the other half of her rescue team. The pastor said, "Laurell, meet George Warren. He helped me the other night, and when he's not rescuing damsels in distress, he plays a mean piano."

"I'm glad to meet you, Mr. Warren," Laurell said. "And thank you for getting me out of that hole."

"You're most welcome," the young man said. "Any time." He stepped back and saluted. "It's about time for me to begin the pre-service music. Otherwise all the guys outside holding down the porch won't know when to come in."

Laurell watched his back retreating and considered what she'd just heard. That people would have to be tolled into the church was something she hadn't expected. Before she could further debate the puzzle, Mr. Warren began to play some of the most beautiful music she'd ever heard, and just as he'd said, suddenly the aisle was full of men of all ages who quickly took seats, filling up the small worship space.

"Here's a bulletin," Mrs. MacCallum whispered, as she handed Laurell a folded piece of paper with a picture of the church on the front. "This will tell you what happens during the service."

I wanted to paint this church. I can use this picture.

She vowed to remember to take the bulletin with her. Then she turned her attention to the service, which included singing songs out of a book, prayers, and at one point, a group of men and women wearing aquamarine robes and sitting behind the pastor rose and sang a song that Laurell had never heard before. But she found the music most beautiful.

Finally, Reverend Lowry rose and spoke for about fifteen minutes. She glanced at the bulletin and saw that the preacher's talk was called a sermon. By the time he finished, Laurell was surprised to realize that she'd actually been engrossed in what he was saying.

She grabbed the bulletin again and read that the sermon had been entitled, "Do You Worship a Full-Service God?"

I've never thought about God doing all that. I wonder why Mama always acted like God took away from you? According to Preacher Bill, God gives us so much.

It was something she would have to think more about. Later. Then before she forgot, Laurell stuck the bulletin into her purse.

It took the two of them forever to make it to the back door of the church and out onto the porch. Or at least it seemed that way to Laurell, who was actually dripping perspiration by the time she was seated in Mrs. MacCallum's van. If there was one single person at church that day who hadn't greeted her and asked how she was doing, Laurell didn't know who it was. It was nice to feel welcome, but it had been exhausting.

"Are we still going by the bed & breakfast?" Mrs. MacCallum asked, as she started the van.

Do I really want to put myself back into the middle of that insanity?

Laurell knew there was a large part of her that simply wanted to go back to Mrs. MacCallum's cabin and take a nap. At the same time, she was truly concerned about her mother. Obviously going there was the only way she was going to discover how things were.

"Do you mind?"

"Not at all. I told you last night we'd go over after church. Just wanted to be sure you hadn't had second thoughts."

"Well, I guess I have been wondering if I really want to do

this. And I'll probably wish later I hadn't. But yeah, I guess I need to check on Mama."

Mrs. MacCallum negotiated the curving mountain roads and they were soon passing between the gateposts. Laurell braced herself for what she knew would undoubtedly be an unpleasant encounter.

In all the time I've been at Mrs. MacCallum's, Mama hasn't called even once. But she had time to talk to the reporters about Russell.

The anticipated unpleasant encounter, however, wasn't to be. Not because Myra Wilson was in a warm and receptive mood, but because she was nowhere to be found. The doors were locked, lights were off inside, and there was no sign that anyone was around.

This place feels deserted. Like a ghost town.

Immediately, she regretted her choice of words, because indeed the air around the inn held no suggestion of life or viability.

"Do you want to go in?" Mrs. MacCallum asked, breaking into Laurell's thoughts.

"I feel like I need to, but I don't have a key. Mama never gave me one." Then a troubling thought occurred. "You don't suppose Mama's in there hurt or something, do you?"

Out of reflex, she tried the front door, only to be jerked back to reality when it resisted her efforts. It was locked, just as she knew it would be. She put her face to the glass in the upper half of the door and cupped her hands around her face to shut out the light, in order to get a better look.

"Are you truly afraid your mother's in there?"

Laurell had never felt so helpless. "I don't know what I think," she wailed. "If I didn't know better, I'd think Mama had closed the inn and walked away."

Unfortunately, I can see her doing exactly that. Especially in the frame of mind she's been in lately.

Then another even more troubling possibility visited itself on her. "Oh, no," Laurell said, struggling to get back the breath that had been unexpectedly stolen from her, "you don't suppose she's in jail, do you?"

"In jail?"

As they stood on the spacious front porch of the deserted bed & breakfast, even the birds that had been so noisy when they'd first driven up seemed to have grasped the severity of the situation. Suddenly everything was quiet, except the thoughts that were bombarding Laurell's mind.

"Yeah, you know what the newspaper said. The police were questioning whether Mama helped Russell escape." Then still another more troubling possibility came to mind. "Or if she's not in jail, has she taken Russell and gone underground with him?"

"Would she do something like that?"

"Truly, I'm afraid she would."

"If she's gone with Russell, she'd have taken her car."

Her car! We need to see if her car's here.

"It would be around back," she told Mrs. MacCallum. "Let's…"

"You stay here," the older woman said. "I can check faster

than you can."

"It's that way," Laurell said, and pointed around to the right side of the inn. "A red Toyota."

In a moment, her friend returned, and Laurell knew by the expression on her face, even before Mrs. MacCallum spoke, that Mama's car was not where it was supposed to be.

"I'm sorry, Laurell. There's no car back there."

If she'd had a place to sit, Laurell would have let her legs collapse, just as they were threatening. Somehow, she understood that would solve nothing, and instead, she tried to steady both her legs and her mind, as she processed what little they knew. Finally, when she'd arrived at a game plan, although it wasn't the plan she wanted, she queried her chauffeur.

"Can we go to the jail? Can we go to Meadeville and talk to the police?"

"Well, sure, if you think we can learn anything?" Mrs. MaCallum extended her arm to connect with Laurell and helped her back to the van.

Laurell's mind was going at warp speed, totally oblivious to the scenery passing by outside the van. Had she been a little bit more observant, she might have realized that her driver was pushing the speed limit. Instead, Laurell was debating how she would ask for information, and what she would do if her mother wasn't in jail.

"What if they won't tell us? What if she isn't under arrest? What do we do then?"

"I don't know," Mrs. MacCallum said, as she concentrated

on safely taking the sharp turns that were so prevalent on the road between Hickory Bend and the county seat. "But let's don't borrow trouble until we have to."

It wasn't long before they had to borrow that trouble.

"No, ma'am, your mother isn't here," the deputy on duty assured Laurell. "In fact, we're looking for her, as well. It would make my job much easier if I could tell you that she's right back there." As if to further emphasize his answer, he pointed with his thumb over his shoulder. Laurell's heart was in her throat as she thanked him.

"Where could she be?" Laurell asked. "It's like she's dropped off the face of the earth."

"We'll find her," the deputy interjected. "You can plan on it. And when we do," he said, leveling a gaze that clearly said, "I'll tolerate no nonsense," on the two women, "she's got some explaining to do. Especially if we find her and your brother together."

Laurell could only imagine how that scenario might go down, and the image that formed in her mind made chills course over her. The deputy's next words only intensified the discomfort.

"Anybody who's assisting them will be in equally as much trouble," he said, as his eyes bored into the both of them. "So if you're really here to find out what we know, so that you can relay that information to them, I'd advise against it."

"You think we're scouting for them? How can you…"

"You're nuts, sonny," Mrs. MacCallum informed him. "But we'll consider ourselves warned." She reached for Laurell's arm. "Come on, we're not going to learn anything else here."

Neither said anything until they were safely in the van and had pulled away from the jail. It was Laurell who broke the silence.

"We have to go back to the inn. Something's wrong, and I'm going to break in if I have to."

Chapter Ten

"What do you expect to find?" the driver asked, as she nosed the van into the first steep curve. "We were just there. Your mother's car wasn't there. The whole place looked deserted."

"I don't know," Laurell said at last, honestly, and admitted to herself that she had to agree. The inn had no sense of life about it at all. "But if I don't go in, I'll always wonder if they're in there, hiding. Mama is so paranoid, I can't put anything past her."

Worse yet, she might be in there, hurt, unable to call for help. Russell might have stolen her car. I wouldn't put that past him.

The van tires squealed coming out of another twisting stretch of road. "Ordinarily, I'd caution against breaking and entering, but in this case, I'm afraid you're right."

Even though Laurell could see that her driver was definitely over the speed limit, it still seemed that the minutes slipped by with the speed of hours. It was as if they would never arrive. Once they did, a quick look around the grounds showed that nothing had changed in the almost two hours they'd been gone.

"So how're you going to get in?" They were standing in the back parking lot, looking up at the second level. "Surely you know some way," Mrs. MacCallum said.

Laurell glanced around the spacious lodge, before looking up in the direction of her bedroom. "If I had two healthy legs," she said, "I could easily climb up to my room." She pointed to the window in question. "It's never locked. I could get in that way."

"If you actually break in," Mrs. MacCallum said, "we'll have to secure whatever way we get inside. Otherwise, we're leaving the B&B vulnerable." She surveyed the inn and her eyes landed on the area of roof that Laurell had indicated. "How would you go about getting up there? If you could climb?"

Laurell pointed out the route she'd use.

"Piece of cake," her companion said. "You're sure the window's unlocked?"

"That's how I left it. But you can't climb up there."

"Watch me," the older woman said, and was already putting one hand over the other, before the words left her mouth.

For the second time in less than two hours, Laurell found herself tied in knots, as she watched the climber slowly move toward her bedroom. At last, Mrs. MacCallum reached the window and began to push. At first, the lower sash wouldn't budge. Had someone locked the window after she left? But why? At last, when Laurell feared that all their efforts were for naught, and began to wonder how they might most expediently break in, she heard the shout of joy.

"I got it," Mrs. MacCallum yelled. "It just wanted to be stubborn."

Relief flooded over Laurell. "Come out of my room, turn left, and you'll be at the main staircase that goes down to the foyer."

"Don't you try to come around to the door without help. It's too rough. I'll come out the front door and come around and get you."

She watched as her partner in crime disappeared through the window, and Laurell began to imagine every step Mrs. MacCallum would take to reach the hallway, the staircase and finally the foyer. "She should be opening the front door right about now," she announced to the deserted parking lot. Laurell watched anxiously for her friend to appear around the end of the building, only to feel the hair on the back of her head stand at attention.

She should have been out by now. What could have happened? A sickening thought suddenly made itself known. *Oh, my, gosh. What if Mama's hiding out in there, and she caught Mrs. MacCallum?*

When she felt that she'd given her friend more than enough time, Laurell was convinced something bad had happened. Contrary to orders, she began to hobble in the direction of the front door, only to meet her missing companion at the corner.

"I told you to stay put until I came for you," Mrs. MacCallum scolded.

"What took you so long?" Laurell wailed. "I was afraid something had happened to you."

"I'm sorry," the older woman said quietly, "I got sidetracked."

Laurell was so relieved that her friend wasn't harmed, she didn't think to follow up on what had delayed Mrs. MacCallum's exit.

With help, Laurell was soon standing in the downstairs foyer, looking up the forbidding staircase she knew there was no way she

187

could navigate. Instead, she decided her voice would have to do the work for her.

In the meantime, her companion had begun to wander the main floor. Laurell could hear her as she called, "Mrs. Wilson! If you're here, show us. We're here to help you."

Laurell was reminded of the warning they'd gotten from the deputy, so she questioned how much help her mother would actually get. Still, she wouldn't automatically turn Myra Wilson over to the authorities.

"Mama!" she called aloud. When there was no response, she screamed, "M A M A! Please answer me."

Deafening silence responded instead and forced her to devise another plan.

"She's not down here," Mrs. MacCallum said. "I've been in every room on this level. In fact, it doesn't look like anyone has been here for several days."

"There's a basement," Laurell said. "And the upstairs, but I can't go up or down."

"No, but I can."

Over the next few minutes, the older woman explored the basement with Laurell standing in the open doorway at the top of the stairs, and they carried on a conversation the entire time. When that search proved futile, Mrs. MacCallum climbed to the second floor, and Laurell provided direction to all the rooms.

"No one up here, either," the older woman said finally, as she stood at the top of the stairs, looking down at Laurell. She hesitated, before adding, "If your mother normally has cosmetics on her vanity and a robe and slippers, they're not there now."

She's left. Without saying anything to me, she just left. But is she with Russell?

"Then she's gone," Laurell said at last. "Her vanity always looks like the cosmetic counter at the department store." Despite her best intentions to the contrary, depression settled over her. Never had she felt so abandoned.

It's like I don't even exist. But that didn't just start. She was that way even before Daddy died.

"We might as well go," she said. "There's nothing more we can do here." Before they left, Laurell reached in the key box and removed a spare key to the front door. "If we have to come back, at least we'll be able to get in."

When Mrs. MacCallum's van pulled into the turnaround at the door to the cabin, Laurell could think of nothing else but her bed. Never mind that she hadn't had lunch. Forget that she needed to put herself into her mother's mind, if there was any hope of finding her. She understood that both her heart and her body had withstood more than she could tolerate.

"I've got to lay down," she announced to Mrs. MacCallum once they were inside. "It feels like I'm going to topple over."

"Don't you even want a sandwich first?"

Mrs. MacCallum was already headed to the kitchen, but stopped when Laurell said, "I couldn't eat a thing right now."

"Then you go on to bed, and we'll have a good meal later

today."

Laurell didn't argue, sure that she wouldn't do anything but lay and stare at the ceiling, worrying about all the problems she had no way to fix. But she was wrong, and the next time she looked at the room around her, it was obvious that it was late in the day.

Oh, dear, I've got to get up. I just meant to rest for a few minutes.

As she clumsily swung her bad leg onto the floor, the fragrance of cooking food assaulted her nose. She couldn't determine what smelled so enticing, but if the aroma was any indication, it was something good.

Turned out while Laurell slept, her hostess had been busy in the kitchen making country-style steak and gravy with mashed potatoes, fried okra, fresh sliced tomatoes and cantaloupe, with peach cobbler and ice cream for dessert.

"How did you know this is my favorite meal," she inquired, when finally she'd spooned up the last of the cobbler. "I mean, this was so good."

"It's one of my favorite meals as well, but I don't ever cook it just for myself. As I've already told you, it's so nice to have company."

While Laurell was glad to be considered a welcomed guest and not a bother, it was also a reminder that she was there because her mother had basically written her off. What other explanation could there be?

As Mrs. MacCallum was clearing the table, she hesitated, put her hand on Laurell's shoulder, and said, "There's something we need to talk about."

At the serious tone in the woman's voice, Laurell felt herself tense up. Was she about to be asked to leave? Never mind that she gave her hostess a chance to cook for two. "Well, sure. Whatever. Have I done something wrong?"

"Wrong? Why ever would you ask that?"

"You sound so serious."

Mrs. MacCallum took a seat next to her guest at the table, reached for her hand, and said, "I need to apologize."

"I don't have the first idea what you mean."

Mrs. MacCallum hesitated, then plunged ahead. "Remember earlier today, when it took me so long to get from the upstairs to the front door?"

"Yeah, I remember. You said you got sidetracked."

"Well what sidetracked me was all those beautiful paintings in your bedroom. You're the artist, right?"

Laurell confessed that she was.

Unwilling to separate herself from what she'd called her passion, she'd made a literal gallery out of her bedroom walls. Being able to awake each morning to the beauty she'd created in a different, happier time, had somehow given her the assurance that someday she would be back behind a paint brush.

That's probably why I love this bedroom so much. It reminds me of home.

"Didn't you see them when you went by the inn to get my stuff?"

"Your mother got those things, and not very graciously, I might add. She wouldn't allow me to even accompany her up to your room."

Why am I not surprised?

"You're good, did you know that?" Mrs. MacCallum slapped her hand on the table top, and the sound caused Laurell to jerk back. "No, make that phenomenal. Your work is exquisite." What surprised Laurell most were the woman's next words. "I should know."

"I finally figured out that I must be pretty good," she confided, "when the art college gave me a half-scholarship. And then I couldn't accept it."

"And you couldn't accept it why?"

She'd shared a little of her past with the older woman, but Laurell realized she hadn't told anyone about all that had gone down, starting when her daddy died. Instead, she'd kept everything boxed up inside herself, and her resentment had continued to grow and poison her mind. It would feel good to unburden herself.

Over the next few minutes, Laurell began with the call that Daddy had suffered a heart attack at his accounting practice and been rushed to the ER. He'd died before any of them could get there, and she'd been denied the chance to tell him that she loved him and to say goodbye.

"It hurts when you don't get that closure you so desperately crave," Mrs. MacCallum said, and Laurell was positive she saw tears in her friend's eyes. "But go on, tell me everything."

Laurell related how each of them had reacted to the drastic change in their lives. "Mama has always been distant, and so busy with her job, but after Daddy died, it was like she built a wall even taller. Nothing that I said made any difference."

"So why did you have to forfeit your scholarship?"

Why did I have to give up all of that possibility? I've never really understood.

"Money, mostly," she said. "And Russell."

At Mrs. MacCallum's confused look, Laurell hurried to explain. "Mama said we couldn't afford to continue living in Atlanta in our home. We had to sell and move where living costs were less. Then Russell got in big trouble, and the judge was willing to cut him some slack, as long as he left the state."

"I see," she said, although Laurell could tell she didn't.

"Mama bought the lodge from a cousin who needed to unload it, and we opened a bed and breakfast."

"But Russell didn't want to come here, so he rebelled."

"Pretty much."

"And what did you do?"

What did I do?

"Well, I guess…" her voice faltered.

"I can tell you what you did. You put all of your needs and your opinions in cold storage, and you tried to make everything work for everyone except yourself. You seeded your own discontent, and you've paid a hefty price, I fear." She hesitated, then said, "By the time I was your age, I was out on my own."

The serious, almost sinister tones of the woman's words caused Laurell to make eye contact.

She is crying. But why?

"You're right," she confessed. "That's exactly what I've done, although I've had to be away from the situation to really see it."

"You should be painting, you know."

Laurell remembered all the pieces on the walls of her room where she was sleeping. Paintings, her hostess had said, that were painted by her daughter. She was about to ask about them again, but remembering the veil of grief that had descended when she'd asked before, she was hesitant to cause any additional pain.

"I would love nothing more than to be in front of my easel with a brush in my hand. One of the things I want to paint is your little church."

"Then you should paint it."

She considered her answer. "Perhaps I will, but right now I've got to find Mama. This is really starting to frighten me."

Curiosity finally overcame her reluctance, and Laurell said, "You seem so adamant that I'm talented. But how can you be so certain?" She bit her tongue and hesitated, before plunging ahead. "I don't mean to open an old wound, but does your opinion have anything to do with the paintings in there?" She pointed toward her bedroom. "Now that artist had true talent."

I can't be crass enough to ask her how she thinks she's an art expert.

As she watched, her friend's eyes puddled with tears again. But the searing grief she'd seen during the earlier conversation was missing.

Finally, the older woman spoke. "My daughter was very talented. It was devastating in so many ways when we lost her."

Laurell couldn't find words to say what her heart dictated and instead wisely kept her mouth shut.

After an uncomfortable period of silence, Mrs. MacCallum found her voice. "You'll just have to take my word for it, but I do know art talent when I see it. God gave you a very special gift, and He expects you to be using it. It just hurts too badly to talk about my daughter."

Unwilling to cause additional discomfort, Laurell changed the conversation back to her mother, although she found the reference to God being the source of her art ability to be interesting. *I've never once thought about where my talents came from.*

"Does she have any friends, either here or back in Atlanta that she might have reached out to?" Mrs. MacCallum said.

I hadn't considered that possibility. Laurell found the question troubling. "She's made no friends here that I know anything about. The inn kept her pretty much confined. But in Atlanta, there was Wanda...." Laurell ran her fingers through her hair. "What was her last name?" Try as she might, Laurell couldn't recall the last name of the woman who had worked at the hotel with Myra.

"Mama and she would pal around outside of the office." She waved her hands. "You know, going shopping, out to eat, stuff like that. But I simply cannot remember her last name. It was kind of funny sounding."

"Do you think your mother might have contacted her?"

"It's worth a shot, but how can I call her if I don't know her name? She might not even have a land line phone, so how would I get her number?"

"Back at the inn, did your mother have an address file, something that might have this woman's contact information?"

"Your guess is as good as mine." Then suddenly, inspiration hit. "If I wait until tomorrow morning, when this Wanda is in the office, I can just call the hotel and ask to be connected with her."

"That's an excellent solution!"

After Mrs. MacCallum had done the dishes, and the women had adjourned to the living room, it took everything Laurell had to keep the conversation away from the taboo subject. Somehow she would have to uncover the answers another way.

If only I had my laptop - but then there's no internet here, so I wouldn't be any better off. Nevertheless, she promised herself that the next time they were out, they'd go by the inn, and Mrs. MacCallum could retrieve it from her bedroom.

When it was finally late enough that she could gracefully retire to her bed without it seeming that she was trying to escape, Laurell began to get ready for the night. She'd just slid between the sheets, desperate for something to occupy herself until it was late enough to go to sleep, when a soft knock sounded.

"Come in."

The door swung open to reveal her hostess, which wasn't a surprise, Laurell decided. What was unexpected were what looked to be scrapbooks clutched in her arms.

"I can't talk about it," Mrs. MacCallum said. "It's just too painful, but you deserve to know why I think you're wasting a God-given talent." She laid the books on the bedside table. "You can read and learn for yourself."

"I didn't mean… mean to pull off a scab. I can do without knowing."

"It's not a deep, dark secret. Brother Bill and several others at the church know, but it's just something I can't revisit."

"If you're sure…"

"I'm sure. Now don't sit up all night reading. You're still recovering you know." She picked up one particular book, the one with a bilious green cover, and laid it in Laurell's lap. "Start with this one."

She took herself out of the room without further discussion, leaving Laurell with a way to answer her questions.

But do I really want to know? Once I do, what difference might it make?

Finally, curiosity overcame caution, and she flipped open the first book. What she saw was a picture cut from a newspaper page of an artist in a gallery with a wall of paintings behind her. The paper was yellowed with age, but it was still readable. At first she didn't see the relevance. A closer inspection, however, caused a connection that felt like an electrical shock.

Mrs. MacCallum! It's her, more than thirty years ago. She's an artist, too?

Her eyes dropped to the caption below the picture to confirm her assumption, where she read, 'Renowned New York artist Mary Elizabeth MacCallum is pictured here at her latest hanging at New York's prestigious Walkaway Gallery. Her one-woman show drew buyers from as far away as Hawaii. Goffrey Walkaway termed her showing as one of the most successful in his gallery's forty year history. "Mark my words," he said, "those who bought paintings during this show have already made money on their investments before they even got them home. Ms. MacCallum's star is just beginning its assent."'

Wow! So if she was so great way back then, what happened?

Laurell finally understood that the answers to her questions were in the pages of the three scrapbooks. A quick assessment told her she'd be reading until the wee hours of the next morning, if she took the time to look at each page. At the same time, she feared if she skipped even a single page, she would miss something important. In the end, she opted for information over rest, never mind that she was still recovering.

I can sleep tomorrow if I have to. But not until after I call Wanda what's-her-name.

It was closer to four o'clock than Laurell was comfortable admitting, when at last she closed the cover on the third and final book of memories. To say that her questions had been answered was an understatement. However, few of the tidbits she's gleaned matched her pre-conceived ideas. That in and of itself only generated more questions.

She turned out the light, glanced at the bedside clock, and mentally calculated the sleep that she might manage to accomplish, and got comfortable. There was a lot of information to digest. And what would she do once she'd processed everything?

How am I supposed to act toward Mrs. MacCallum, now that I know everything?

As blissful sleep claimed her, Laurell drifted off, weighing what she'd learned. Mary Elizabeth MacCallum had been one of the nation's leading artists. Buyers from around the globe snatched up her finished pieces as fast as she could turn them out. Her landscapes were rich in detail and glowed with an inner light that the critics couldn't explain, even while they were in awe of her talent.

Her only child, a daughter named Muriel, it seemed, had inherited her mother's talent squared many times over, the critics had proclaimed. Mother and daughter had become a two-person painting team, and had hung their work in some of the most distinguished shows and galleries in the country.

Through it all, when questioned, Mrs. MacCallum had been quick to give all the credit for their talents and success to God. He, she maintained in every article Laurell had read, was the source of their abilities. At the height of their success, tragedy had struck.

Muriel was diagnosed with cancer, a rapidly spreading form. Mrs. MacCallum had moved them to Hickory Bend, where she'd had a cabin for several years. From there, they would be close to one of the nation's leading cancer treatment centers. It had proven to be too little, too late. Muriel had been so distraught over her mother's refusal to accept her terminal diagnosis, that when she was told there was nothing more that could be done for her, Muriel had exhausted the last of her energy to run away from home. She was found by search parties the next day, in the woods. Death came hours later.

Mrs. MacCallum had, according to one of the last articles, retreated into herself and refused to ever pick up a paint brush again. "God has stolen from me the most precious thing I had, and I've lost the will to paint," she'd said in one article. Despite pleas from the public and art professionals, she'd stuck to that vow, and had even sold all of the paintings in her inventory. The only pieces she kept were the paintings Muriel had done before she got sick.

Those are the paintings in this room. Gosh, I'm sleeping in the presence of greatness. It must have been very traumatic for her to find me in the woods and hurt like that.

What would she do, how should she act, when she had to sit across the breakfast table from the woman who had been so kind?

Chapter Eleven

When the aromas of breakfast cooking first roused her the next morning, Laurell couldn't understand why it felt as if she hadn't rested. It was as if she hadn't been asleep for more than a few minutes. Slowly the light bulb began to glow, and much too quickly, the enormity of all she'd learned in those darkest hours of the night returned.

I've got to get up. I just don't know how I can face this woman who's been so good to me.

As she hobbled her way to the breakfast table, Laurell's mind was twirling and tumbling. Should she acknowledge the scrapbooks, or did she wait for Mrs. MacCallum to mention them? Did she simply say "thank you" and let it go at that, or should she offer her sympathy, even though it had been thirty years since the daughter's death?

Mrs. MacCallum must be older than she looks, because it's been thirty years since her daughter died, and she was just about my age. That would make her at least in her early seventies.

In the end, all the indecision was taken from her, and everything went in a different direction.

The sound of a vehicle approaching the cabin made Laurell turn and look in that direction, even though she wasn't where she could peep out the window. It was early for visitors, even in the mountains.

"Someone's coming, Mrs. MacCallum." She could see the other woman working over the stove.

"I'll get it," Mrs. MacCallum said as she hurried through the room, wiping her hands on her apron as she made her way to the door. Before she got there, a strident knocking alerted both of them that this rare visitor was there on business.

"Good morning," she said, as she swung open the door to reveal a uniformed deputy standing on the other side.

"Deputy Walker, Ma'am, from the Meadeille Police Department. I need to speak with Miss Laurell Wilson."

What do they want with me? The other deputy told us we could get in trouble for helping Mama and Russell, but we haven't done anything. We still don't know where they are.

"She's right here," Mrs. MacCallum said to the officer. "Won't you come in?"

While she'd stood there frightened, wondering what was about to happen, Matilda had come up quietly beside her, and put her snout in Laurell's hand. It was one of the many ways the precious dog, who had helped to rescue her, had comforted Laurell in the days she'd been at the cabin. She took heart in the dog's compassion.

The officer removed his hat, entered the cabin, and when he spotted Laurell hunched over her walker, he said, "You would be Miss Wilson, I assume." Only there was no question in his voice.

"I am." She wanted to say more, but those two words were all that would leave her mouth.

"Won't you have a seat?" Mrs. MacCallum invited.

The officer ignored the offer and instead said, "When were you last at your mother's B&B?"

"Yesterday afternoon," Laurell replied. "Why?"

"And how did you gain entry?"

The two women exchanged glances, but both knew the other had nothing to hide, and Laurell caught her hostess's signal to answer the question.

"I didn't have a door key. Mrs. MacCallum climbed up to my second floor bedroom window and entered that way. I never lock that window. Then she let me in through the front door." She indicated her leg in the brace and the walker. "There was no way I could climb."

"But you didn't break in?"

Again, a glance went back and forth between the two women.

"No sir. Mrs. MacCallum went through the window to keep from having to break in and then have to repair the damage."

"And what all did you find once you got inside?"

Laurell wasn't sure where this man's questioning was going, and she hesitated, fearful of giving the wrong answer.

"Basically nothing," she said at last. "We didn't find Mama in there hurt, and we didn't find Russell."

"You went through the entire place?"

"Between us, we did," Mrs. MacCallum interposed. "The basement, the main level, and the second floor. No one was there and nothing was out of order." She regarded him quizzically and then added, "Laurell is staying here because there are no bedrooms on the ground floor at the inn. As you can see, she can't climb stairs."

Well, if you don't count Mama's things being gone, nothing was out of order.

"Now suppose you tell us why we're being questioned like this so early in the morning." Mrs. MacCallum's words weren't ugly, but Laurell heard a bluntness she hadn't seen in this woman before.

"This is police business, ma'am, and I ask the questions."

"And this is my house, and unless you have a warrant which you haven't produced, entitling you to be here, I suggest you tell us what's brought you all the way from Meadeville before breakfast." She moved to better face the man. "We're not adversaries here, you know."

Instead of responding to her entreaty directly, the officer fired back yet another question. "So you left the inn at what time yesterday?"

"Two-forty-five roughly."

"You checked the time before you left? Did you think you might have to account for your actions?"

"It was nothing like that," Mrs. MacCallum said. "When you walk in my back door, there's a huge schoolhouse clock on the opposite wall." She pointed toward the kitchen. "You're welcome to go see for yourself." When he didn't respond, she said, "It read two-fifty-nine when we walked in the door, and it takes roughly fifteen minutes from the inn to here." She regarded him with what Laurell could only describe as a no-nonsense look. "But I'm sure you already know how long it takes."

Again ignoring their questions, he said, "And you didn't go back after that?"

"No," both women said in unison, as if on cue. Mrs. MacCallum continued, "We've been right here ever since."

The officer said nothing, but shifted his gaze from one woman to the other, as if he had the power to penetrate their skin and determine if they were telling the truth. Finally he said, "And you didn't break a pane in the kitchen back door to gain entrance?"

"No," Laurell said. "We did not. Like I told you, we saw that as an option, but knew it would have to be repaired."

Is that what this is all about?

"I'm assuming, then, deputy, that there is now a broken pane of glass in that door?"

"There is. What's more, the kitchen has been rifled through for certain. We can't be sure about anything else."

Their conversation was interrupted by the smell of something burning, and Mrs. MacCallum hastily excused herself and headed back toward the kitchen.

Sudden inspiration hit. "Give me just a minute officer. I'm kinda slow with this thing." Laurell returned to her room and was soon back dangling a key from her fingers. "Here, officer. I got a door key before we left yesterday, so there would be no need to break in or climb back up to my bedroom window." She offered him the key, which he ignored. "You're welcome to take it and check it. All the outside doors are keyed alike."

"Did your brother have a key?"

"I really don't know."

Mama never gave me a key, but I'm betting Russell had one.

An idea occurred to her. "You took all of his possessions when he was arrested. Did he have a key on him?"

From the sour expression on his face, I'd guess that's one thing they didn't check.

After a few more back and forth questions and answers, the officer left, but not before warning them to stay clear of the property. Laurell was left to process all she'd finally learned. It seemed that law enforcement was checking the B&B every four or five hours to see if there was any sign of Russell or Myra. When the officer on patrol had checked at six o'clock that morning, he'd found the back door standing open, and the kitchen ransacked.

"We must have made our visit between their checks," Mrs. MacCallum said. "It never occurred to me that we might have gotten caught."

"Well, we weren't doing anything wrong. That is still my home."

It was also a home she was suddenly concerned about, in more ways than one.

I can't believe that Mama just locked the inn and walked off. We had reservations booked at least three weeks ahead. Never mind the revenue from the lunch trade.

"Mrs. MacCallum, they're assuming that Russell broke in to get food. But what if it was a homeless person? What if it was someone else and they went on through and stole stuff to sell?"

"You make a good point."

"But just because we think it's valid, doesn't mean the police have considered that."

"Then perhaps we need to make sure they do," her hostess said. "Let's get breakfast and get ready for the day." She rose and headed back to the kitchen. "We're going to Meadeville."

It wasn't until they were eating breakfast, taking little time for conversation, when Laurell remembered her phone call.

"I'm supposed to call Wanda this morning. I'd almost forgotten."

"In all the confusion, I had, too. But you probably need to make that call before we leave. It might have a bearing on what we tell the police."

While the older woman put away the breakfast leftovers, Laurell headed to the phone. Fortunately, she'd called her mother's employment number enough down through the years that she still had it in memory.

"Dawsonville Suites Hotel, how may I direct your call?"

Laurell hesitated, almost reluctant to speak to Wanda. What if she didn't know anything about her mother? Worse yet, what if she did?

"I need to speak with Wanda, please."

"We have two employees named Wanda."

That was a wrinkle she hadn't foreseen.

"This Wanda works in contract sales."

At least I hope that's still her job. What if she doesn't work there at all? It's been a year.

"That would be Wanda Sbrowski. One moment, please."

That's her! I knew she had an unusual last name.

After several rings, Laurell heard a voice on the other end. "This is Wanda Sbrowski. How may I help you?"

Now that she actually had the woman on the phone, Laurell suddenly found herself tongue-tied.

"Hello. This is Wanda. Is anyone there?"

"This is Laurell Wilson, Ms. Sbrowski." At the last minute she'd remembered that Wanda was divorced and did not like being called 'Mrs.' " I'm Myra Wilson's daughter."

"Yes, Laurell. You're the last person I expected to hear from this morning." After a pause, she said, "Nothing's wrong, I hope."

"That's just it," Laurell replied. "That's what I'm trying to determine. Mama's missing and I was hoping you might have heard from her."

"Well…. why are you asking?"

She knows something.

"Ms. Sbrowski, if you know anything about Mama, please tell

me. There's just a lot going on here and we need to try to help her."

"But I promised…"

"You promised her you wouldn't give her away. So you have talked to her."

"When I make a promise, I…"

Laurell knew she had to convince the woman to tell what she knew. "Wanda, if you truly want to help Mama, you'll tell me what you know."

"Your mother called me about five days ago and said the constant stress of running the bed and breakfast was getting to her, and that she needed to get away for a few days. I told her to come stay with me."

"Mama's at your house?"

"She came that same day. But you're right, Laurell. Something is wrong she isn't herself."

As much as she rejoiced to know where her mother was, Laurell was troubled by the report she was getting. "What do you mean? How isn't she herself?"

Her question was met with dead silence. "Ms. Sbrowski, you're my mother's best friend. If you care about her, you'll tell me what's going on. All I want to do is help her." Laurell realized her voice had taken on a pleading tone, but the insanity had gone on too long.

"She's defeated," Ms. Sbrowski said. "There's no fight left in her. In truth, I'm questioning if she hasn't gone off the deep end."

"Mentally, you mean?"

"Mentally and physically. All she does it sit and stare at the wall."

"You mean she hasn't left your house since she got there?"

"Oh, no. She's gone some. At least a couple of times a day, she's gone for an hour or so. Usually mid-morning, and again mid-afternoon. But then she comes back and sits on the couch. She doesn't even watch TV."

As Mrs. MacCallum came back through the room, Laurell flashed her a thumbs-up. "Thanks for your help this morning," she said to her source of information. "I'd appreciate it if you wouldn't tell Mama we've talked."

"Oh, you don't have to worry about that. I wouldn't want to be on the bad side of Myra Wilson."

"Thanks, Ms. Sbrowski. If anything changes, would you please let me know?"

Wanda Sbrowski said she would, and Laurell gave her Mrs. MacCallum's phone number.

"She's in Atlanta?"

"She's in Atlanta, Mrs. MacCallum. And I've got a sneaking suspicion that Russell is with her."

"At her friend's house?"

"No, Russell wasn't mentioned." She shared what she'd learned about her mother's behavior and actions. "I think she has Russell hidden out somewhere close by. Taking him with her to

Wanda's would have required too many explanations." She went on to relate Myra's frequent absences.

"She's leaving the house and going somewhere. That's the only scenario that makes sense."

As if she were reading Laurell's mind, Mrs. MacCallum said, "How long does it take to get to Atlanta?"

Laurell told her. "Then we'd best get on the road."

Three and a half hours later, they pulled up at the address where Wanda Sbrowski had lived for as long as Laurell had known of her. There, in the drive, sporting North Carolina license plates, was Myra's red Toyota.

"We found her," Laurell said. "And obviously, she's there right now."

But now what do we do?

Mrs. MacCallum echoed Laurell's unspoken question. "Do we confront her now, here? Or do we wait until she goes out again and follow her?"

Laurell debated the issue before finally saying, "It's just twelve-thirty. There's no telling how long we'd have to sit here. And I don't know this part of town that well. We might lose her if we try to tail her." She hesitated another moment and then said, "I say we go in now."

It was one of those moments that cameras were invented to capture. The look of sheer shock, quickly replaced by an expression of abject terror on Myra's face, was how the two visitors were greeted when the door opened.

"La... Laurell... what? How?"

As if she'd suddenly realized she was caught, Myra shoved the door shut, but Mrs. MacCallum was too fast for her. With her foot wedged in the door, and by pushing together, Laurell and her traveling partner gained entry.

Had the situation been otherwise, Laurell would think later, she might have been able to feel some compassion, some sympathy for her mother. As it was, Myra's refusal to face facts had already cost too much. It had to end. Here and now, things had to turn around.

"Stop, Mama," she ordered in a voice she didn't know she had within her. "You've run as far as you're going to run."

As if in shock, Myra Wilson stood rooted to where she was. "You don't talk to me like that, young lady."

"Yes, I do. Mama, you need help and that's what you're going to get. Before this insanity goes on another minute." She reached to take her mother's hand, but that hand was withdrawn. "Well, at least you've still got some fight left in you."

Over the next hour, amid many screams of anger and frustration, and tears on the part of all three women, the truth finally came to the surface. Laurell was astounded to learn just how bad things were. And there was little satisfaction in knowing that her hunch had been correct. Myra hadn't assisted Russell to escape, but when he sought her out, she'd sheltered him and left the state with him. Just as Laurell had suspected, Myra was hiding him in a cheap motel a few blocks away. She would go twice a day to buy food and take it to him.

"But Laurell," she wailed, once the truth was finally on the table. "Your brother says everything that's happened to him is my fault. And all I've ever wanted to do was protect him."

"By not allowing him to be responsible for his own actions," Mrs. MacCallum said, quietly, "you gave him an inflated sense of importance and invincibility."

"But I love him so much."

You openly profess your love for my brother. You do nothing but criticize me.

"Then you need to make him give himself up to the police. He's in so much more trouble because he escaped and ran away." Laurell hated the prospect of hurting her mother further, but Russell couldn't live on the run forever. At some point, he would be caught. Getting her mother to do the right thing was another matter entirely.

I have to agree with Wanda. Mama isn't totally rational.

Among other pieces of information that had come out of the bleeding of emotions earlier was the true status of the B&B. They were behind with the mortgage, Myra had shared, and despite pleas to her cousin - it didn't appear the sought after extension would be granted.

"He told me when I bought the place that he was so glad to get it off his hands, that the money was secondary. Now he's singing a different tune, and if I don't come up with three payments by next week, he'll begin foreclosure."

"If we can give him one payment now, surely he'll work with us on the rest."

Even that may be difficult to manage, since we've been closed for at least a week. We're sure to have a whole lot of angry customers out there. Word of mouth won't be good.

"I tried that," Myra said, through the tears that tracked down her face. "He was so cruel. It's three months or nothing. He'll foreclose. You can count on it."

The realization that they might be losing the only home they had was as infuriating as it was frightening. That her mother could have been so irresponsible was equally troubling.

"The money, Mama. Where did the money go? We had a good business going and we were making enough to pay the bills. How could you just not pay the mortgage?" It was all she could do to contain her anger. "Did we truly not have the money? Or did you spend it on something else?"

Please let me be wrong. Although the sick feeling in the pit of her stomach told her she already knew the answer, Laurell had to hear the words out of her mother's mouth.

"I had to hold some money back in case Russell needed it. Lawyers don't come cheap."

Laurell felt Mrs. MacCallum's hand on her shoulder and knew that her friend understood the anger that her mother's words had triggered.

"Mrs. Wilson," Mrs. MacCallum said, "I've always hesitated to put myself into things that didn't concern me, but I don't think you understand. You have two children, not just Russell. I've already seen enough from you to know that you've discarded your daughter with not one thought to her welfare."

Myra half-rose from where she sat, then as if the air had been sucked from her, she collapsed back into her chair.

"I resent that!" Her eyes crackled as she surveyed the woman leveling the charges. "And you are exactly right. This is absolutely none of your business."

Laurell's mouth flew into action, and she was helpless to stop the words that spilled out. "At least Mrs. MacCallum's concerned about me," she charged, and saw her mother react as if she'd taken a head-on hit. "You will not talk to her in that manner. If she hadn't driven me here to find you, I still wouldn't know where my mother was."

Myra dropped her head, but said nothing. Silence reigned supreme and Laurell wondered what she could say next. Then the thought of losing the inn brought her back to the most immediate problem.

"What about Daddy's life insurance money? You couldn't have paid the mortgage with that?"

"But that's for our future," Myra protested. "I couldn't use that for living expenses."

"But you could use it to pay for lawyers and bail money, which Russell totally threw away?"

Myra puffed up, again. "That's different. Somebody had to help him."

Laurell had heard all she was willing to hear. It was time to get serious.

"Let me tell you something, Mama. All of this comes to a

screeching halt today. Right now."

"You can't tell me what to do."

"I just did, Mama. And I'm about to do it again."

"What… what do you mean?"

She chose to answer the question with a question. "Where's Russell, Mama? Where do you have him hidden?"

"I'm not going to tell you."

"Oh, yes, you are. Otherwise, I'm going to turn you in to the Meadeville police and you can do some jail time alongside your precious son."

"Jail? Me? Whatever for?"

"Mama. Where is your common sense? You not only gave assistance to an escapee, you sneaked him across state lines and provided shelter for him. You're so guilty there's no way you'll escape jail time."

"She's telling the truth," Mrs. MacCallum offered up softly, in tones that were soft and non-threatening. "The sooner you make a U-turn in this situation, the better off you and Russell both will be."

It took quite a while longer before they were able to wear down Myra's resistance. Finally, she gave up the name of the motel and the room number. Laurell wasted no time in placing a call to the police in North Carolina. By the time she ended the call, she'd provided the information on where they could find Russell. She had also assured them that Myra was on her way to surrender herself.

"It will take us four or five hours to get there, but we're

coming."

She hadn't told the police, but her plan was to hang back and be certain that the local police had Russell in custody, before they left Atlanta.

Mama, please forgive me for what I've done. It was necessary, if we were ever to straighten out this mess.

Chapter Twelve

T he next few hours were as heartbreaking as they were hectic. Laurell had hesitated to allow Mrs. MacCallum to make the long drive back alone. At the same time, after the way Myra had reacted to the team of officers they observed take Russell into custody on behalf of the out-of-state police, Laurell knew she dared not trust her mother to drive herself back.

In the state she's in, she'll either wreck and kill herself, or she'll take off once she gets behind the wheel, and we'll never find her.

"It's okay," Mrs. MacCallum had said, when Laurell offered her apologies. "You need to be with your mother. In fact, you really need to be behind the wheel, except with your right leg in that brace, you can't drive. Your mother needs emotional help." She hugged Laurell in a gesture of sincere concern. "I'll be praying all the way. You can count on that."

Unfortunately, Laurell had to agree. The more they were together, the more she observed her mother, the more she understood that something had snapped. How difficult putting all that to rights would be, she was afraid to guess. They had parked Mrs. MacCallum's van well clear of the motel room where Russell was staying. Laurell had figured her brother would recognize Myra's red Toyota, so they'd left it behind at Wanda's.

It had all been over within a matter of a couple of minutes.

The police had arrived with six officers, guns drawn, and had moved quickly to the door to room one-seventy-one. When Myra had seen the guns, she'd lost it, and it had taken both of the other two to keep her from bolting the van to rescue her son. When Russell was brought out in handcuffs, Mrs. MacCallum had pulled up beside the patrol car, where he'd been placed in the back seat.

Laurell noted that he was in a highly agitated state that was only made worse when Myra emerged from the back of the van, and Russell realized that she'd given him up to the police. It was a mother and son reconciliation she didn't think she would ever forget.

"You're not my mother!" the prisoner had screamed in a manner that gave every suggestion of someone who had come completely apart at the seams. "I hate you! Do you hear me? I HATE YOU! Don't you ever come around me again! YOU'RE NOT MY MOTHER!"

When they realized how totally destroyed Myra was following that verbal altercation, the two ladies had made a simultaneous executive decision.

"Let's go back and get your mother's luggage out of her car. We're all going back together, in this van, and I'm going to drive."

"We'll find some way to get Mama's car back tomorrow."

Laurell didn't know right at that moment how she would accomplish that, but there was no way her mother could be trusted behind the wheel. As it turned out, they were well out of Georgia and only about an hour away from their destination, before Myra came out of her hysterics to notice how they were traveling.

Laurell had called Wanda Sbrowski as they were leaving

Atlanta and brought her up to speed. "I wanted you to know what's gone down, and why Mama's car is still in your driveway but she's with me."

"Oh, Laurell, I knew something was wrong, but I never, ever could have dreamed it was something this bad. Please keep me posted."

Laurell promised she would, then turned her attention to other equally pressing matters. It took a good bit of wrangling, but she finally got from her mother the name and contact information of the cousin who held the mortgage. She would call him and try to negotiate a way around losing the inn to foreclosure.

I resented being made to feel like an indentured servant at the B&B, but neither do I want us to lose it. First, however, I've got to get Mama settled and squared away with the police.

What that would take, Laurell wasn't sure. Neither was she comfortable with just handing her mother over. She might have been guilty of aiding and abetting an escapee, but she also needed some professional emotional help. Getting the police to recognize that need would be the problem.

The closer to home they got, the more troubled her mind became. Turning Myra over to the police before she saw a doctor would almost guarantee that her mother would get no medical attention. Myra had retreated into herself, and was quiet and still in the back seat, almost in the fetal position.

"Mama needs to see a doctor as soon as possible. I simply cannot give her over to the police without a doctor in attendance," she said in a low whisper, hoping their passenger wouldn't overhear.

"I agree. Let me see what I can do."

Laurell couldn't imagine how Mrs. MacCallum could pull a doctor out of thin air, but she also knew her friend was a most innovative person. She would just have to trust that there was a way.

"I'm going to pull over at this convenience store," her driver said. "I need to get some gas anyway."

Fearful that her mother would realize that the van had stopped and try to escape, Laurell sat at full attention, while Mrs. MacCallum left the driver's seat and moved to the nearest gas pump. In a few minutes, she reclaimed the wheel and Laurell breathed a giant sigh of relief as they began moving again. Myra was out of it and was none the wiser.

"It's handled," she whispered to Laurell, who had to tamp down the embers of curiosity that begged to know exactly how it had been handled. But the less said at that point, the better. If her friend said it was handled, she'd just have to have confidence that it was.

Less than forty-five minutes later the van was pulled beneath the portico of the Meadeville Memorial Hospital, near the ER entrance, and two men approached. One of them looked strangely familiar, and after a moment, Laurell realized it was George Warren, the pianist from Mrs. MacCallum's church. With him, looking like an older version of Mr. Warren, was a man in a white coat, carrying a standard issue medical bag.

The doctor entered through the sliding door of the van, and after asking the other two women to leave, he began to speak to Myra and take her blood pressure and pulse, and listen to her chest. When he exited a few minutes later, Laurell held her breath, almost afraid to hear his verdict.

What if he doesn't think Mama's sick enough to need help?

She needn't have worried. When the doctor approached them, his face was grave. During the time they'd been standing outside the van, Laurell had learned that the man was indeed George Warren's brother. Mrs. MacCallum had called Pastor Bill, who'd gotten hold of George, who'd sent out an SOS to his brother.

"Mrs. Wilson is in desperate need of emotional treatment. Once we would have said she'd had a nervous breakdown. I'd certify that even if she wasn't facing arrest. There's no way she can be locked away in a cell right now."

"So what do we do?" Laurell was relieved to know that someone qualified agreed that Myra was in a bad way. At the same time, how were they to fight the police?

"Does she have an attorney?" the doctor asked.

"She hired one for my brother before he escaped, but I don't think she has an attorney of her own. And my brother's lawyer will probably deny even knowing her. She was pretty rough on him the last time they talked. And then Russell escaped."

"I see what you mean." The doctor looked at his younger brother. "George. What about Peter McComb that goes to church with you?"

"But he handles business law," George said in protest.

"At this point, a lawyer's a lawyer. See if you can reach him."

George withdrew a few feet away and when he returned, he

said, "Peter will meet us at the police station in about fifteen minutes. He assumes you just want him to represent Mrs. Wilson long enough for you to certify that she needs to be hospitalized, and for him to insist that she be booked and released to an appropriate facility."

"That Peter's as smart as I thought he was."

They waited a full fifteen minutes, before Mrs. MacCallum started the van and they backtracked the six blocks to the police station. The doctor and George followed in George's car, and when they pulled into a vacant parking space out front, Mrs. MacCallum said, "There's Peter." She pointed to a man standing near the front entrance, attaché case hanging from his hand.

As Laurel made to help her mother out of the van, the doctor was alongside. "Let me get her, but you're going to need to pay Lawyer McComb a retainer." At the look of horror on her face, he chuckled. "I'd say a dollar would be adequate in this case. He can bill you for the balance."

Ashamed to admit she didn't even have a dollar on her, Laurell was both relieved and embarrassed when George Warren shoved a dollar bill into her hand. "You can owe me."

We owe three months mortgage payments, and now we're going to owe Dr. Warren, the lawyer, and now George as well. This is going to get expensive in a hurry.

Laurell hurried ahead of the doctor and Mrs. MacCallum, who were slowly walking Myra into the police station. Her mother's lack of fight over what was to come was proof plenty that mentally she'd snapped.

Oh, Mama, we've just got to get you well.

She made quick work of conferring with the attorney, paying him the requisite retainer, and following everyone into the station. The police were less than thrilled that their anticipated prisoner had shown up with lawyer and doctor in tow. When they learned that Dr. Warren wanted to place Myra Wilson in a psychiatric unit in an Asheville hospital, instead of in one of their guest suites, they were incensed.

"Let me tell you how it is," Dr. Warren informed them. "I'm prepared to certify that this woman isn't capable of answering for her actions or defending herself under questioning. Lawyer McComb here is prepared to go before a judge tonight and get a court order that will supersede your jurisdiction."

"This is highly irregular," the officer in charge protested. "This woman assisted an escapee to avoid capture. That's more serious than a traffic ticket."

"And if she were in a mental position to adequately answer to the charges, I wouldn't be recommending that she be confined to a mental facility for the short term."

Laurell saw the officer's face falter and took hope that things would go their way.

"Let me be honest, Officer. If you insist on placing this sick woman in a cell, I'm prepared to get on the witness stand and testify as a medical professional that she was denied treatment she desperately needed to adequately participate in her own defense. The judge will throw the case out of court so quickly, you won't see it fly by. And then Mrs. Wilson and her family can sue the police department."

The look that the officer gave the doctor would have curdled milk, Laurell decided. But it also led to a very poor surrender.

"Fine. We'll release her to a mental hospital, but there are conditions."

Laurell held her breath.

"We book her right now, take her fingerprints and mug shot, and she travels under arrest to the hospital in an ambulance." He surveyed those in the room. "That's my offer. Take it or leave it and we'll take our chances in court."

Is this a good thing or a bad? I can't tell by looking at either the doctor or the lawyer.

"Get her booked," the doctor ordered. He turned to the attorney. "Mr. McComb, would you please call for an ambulance for your client. Tell them we're going to Mercy Hospital in Asheville."

"Mercy is one of the best psychiatric hospitals in the country," he offered, as explanation to those assembled.

With both the doctor and the attorney in attendance, Myra was escorted to the back of the building, and within just a few minutes, the ambulance attendants entered the lobby pushing a gurney.

"We're here for a run to Mercy."

"For my mother," Laurell volunteered. "They've got her in the back right now."

"We can wait," the driver said. "In the meantime, I need to get some information from you."

He pulled out a laptop computer, opened it, and began to fire questions. By the time they brought Myra back to the front, her daughter had provided all the needed information and had signed a guarantee of payment, subject to insurance.

The tab for this just continues to grow. I don't even want to know what this ambulance trip will cost.

They watched Myra being loaded into the back of the ambulance that took off with lights flashing, but, thankfully, Laurell thought, there was no siren.

"I've already put in a call to a doctor at Mercy who is top-notch," Dr. Warren advised. "His name's Dr. Penney, and he'll be waiting for her to arrive."

"And as soon as we can, we'll get over to see her," Laurell said.

She saw the doctor's face contort and sensed that she wouldn't like what would come next.

"Sorry, Miss Wilson. Your mother won't be allowed to have visitors for probably a week to ten days. Standard procedure." He wiped his brow and continued, "And in this case, the police will probably have a say-so on who can see her and when."

I forgot. Mama's under arrest even in the hospital. Oh, well.

"And you'll need to arrange for other legal representation for her," the attorney added. "I was glad to help today. Obviously your mother was in need of immediate intervention, but this is a little out of my league."

"Thank you, so much," Laurell told him. "You saved us. I'll call your office in the morning with billing information."

He agreed and made a quick exit, leaving the doctor and his brother, Mrs. MacCallum, and Laurell standing on the sidewalk.

"We'll be going as well," the Warren brothers said.

Laurell hugged both of them and offered her thanks.

When it was just the two women, Laurell said, "I can't believe you could just make a couple of phone calls and bring all these people out of the woodwork."

"All I did was call my church family. That's what a family does. They look after each other."

I never realized that churches did all of that. But I didn't have any way to know.

"I guess we can head back to your place."

"Are you all right?" The question was blunt, but compassionate. "You've had a lot thrown at you today."

"I'm sure it will all hit me later, but right now, I'm as well as I'm going to be. But at some point soon, I've got to get into the B&B."

"The policeman this morning told us to stay clear."

Without answering, Laurell turned on her heel and strode back into the police station, where she confronted the officer who had just lost face.

"Yes, Miss Wilson?"

"The deputy who visited me this morning said I can't go back into the B&B. But there are some business and insurance papers that I'm going to need no later than tomorrow morning."

"And you expect us to do what? Go in and get them for you?"

She wanted to respond to the snide tone in his question, but bit back the words that struggled to overpower her mouth. "I'm simply asking if it's necessary that the inn still be considered a crime scene, since you have my mother, and my brother is under arrest in Georgia. Obviously, whoever broke in was only looking for food."

He appeared to be studying her question. Finally, when she felt tempted to call Lawyer McComb to come back, the officer said, "I'll have someone take down the crime scene tape in the morning. But that's the best I can do."

"Thank you," she said, and again bit back what she knew she didn't need to say. She turned to leave, and remembered. "What about my brother? Where is he and what will happen with him?"

He glanced at the clock. "My officers should be picking him up from the Atlanta police about now. When he gets here, he'll be in the cell back there where your mother should be."

"Will I be able to visit him?"

Not that I'm really anxious to face his venom again any time soon. Something tells me he won't have cooled down any.

"That remains to be seen. You'll need to coordinate with his attorney." He hesitated, as if he was debating whether to say more. "You might want to put in a call to Gene Taylor. He was your brother's last attorney, but I think he bailed." For the first time, Laurell intercepted what she interpreted as a look of sympathy. "He's going to need a really good lawyer, you know."

Laurell added that chore to the list that was already getting top-heavy. The next day would be very busy. But first on the list would be securing the bed and breakfast against foreclosure. Russell would just have to wait his turn.

Even though she assured Mrs. MacCallum that she wasn't hungry, her hostess insisted that she herself was starving. A stop at one of the town's most popular take-out places resulted in two bags of food to go. Laurell saw immediately there was too much for just one person. Later, after she'd eaten to her heart's content, she was thankful that her friend hadn't paid her protests any mind.

They spent the evening going over all Laurell had to accomplish the next day, which turned out to be a more lengthy list than she'd imagined.

"Oh, gosh, how am I ever going to get all of this handled?"

"The same way you eat an elephant," Mrs. MacCallum advised. "One bite at a time gets the job done."

"Yeah, but where do I take the first bite? Remember, you're going to have to drive me wherever I have to go."

The image of her mother's red car still parked in Atlanta suddenly sprang into her mind. "Oh, shoot, I'd totally forgotten about getting the car back." She viewed her brace with a critical eye. "Not that I could drive it if I had it here." Her promise to keep Wanda informed popped into her mind. Rather than add yet one more item to an already top-heavy to-do list for the next day, she reached for the phone.

"I'll call her right now."

"Tell her we can come back for the car day after tomorrow."

As much as she appreciated Mrs. MacCallum's offer, the thought having to make another long distance round-trip in one day was almost depressing.

By the time she and Wanda ended their conversation, Laurell had shared about Myra's arrest and hospitalization, and how all of that had transpired. Wanda, on the other hand, had volunteered to bring the car back to Hickory Bend the next day.

"I've got three days off, starting tomorrow. There's nothing I'd love more than to get out of town and just get away. My sister will follow me in my car, and we'll go on vacation for a couple of days."

"That would definitely take a big ticket item off my list. I'm just sorry I can't offer to host you at the inn, but I'm not sure what will have to be done before we can have guests again."

If we're fortunate enough to still have guests after all the bad PR we've probably gotten.

Laurell climbed in the bed that night more exhausted, mentally and physically, than she ever remembered being. When the sun finally rousted her out the next morning, she felt as if the proverbial truck had run her down, reversed, and come back for a second pass. But there were things to be done, and none of it would happen if she slept in.

Following a quick breakfast and clean-up, she and Mrs. MacCallum were soon at the B&B, where the offending yellow and black tape that had barred them entry was missing.

Laurell said, "The officer may think that I should check in with him before we go in, but he's got another think coming. This place is no more an active crime scene than I am!"

They were soon inside, and Laurell was struck anew with the deathly silence that permeated the place. Even from day one there had been people coming and going. She'd never known the big lodge to be so quiet and lacking personality.

Will we ever be able to revive our business? We won't if we don't have an inn to rent out.

Laurell's first item of business was to make contact with their lienholder, because time truly was of the essence. And if she didn't act quickly, her bravado would desert her. This man was a cousin of her mother's, but she'd never even laid eyes on him.

"Wouldn't know him if he walked in the door right now," she explained to Mrs. MacCallum, who had gone through her mother's little office, while Laurell stood at the bottom of the stairs telling her where to look. It was cumbersome doing it that way, but she couldn't climb the stairs, and she needed all the paperwork at her fingertips before she placed the call.

For the first ten minutes of her one-sided conversation with Roger Justice, whom she judged from the sound of his voice to be a man in his fifties, she felt like she was drowning in quicksand. She had to listen as he droned on about how many other people had been beating down his door to buy the inn, but because Myra was family, he'd let her have it.

I distinctly remember Mama saying that he hadn't had any nibbles on the property, and was overjoyed when she wanted to buy it. But it won't get me anywhere to dispute what he says.

The next ten minutes, she heard his opinion of people who didn't live up to their word and welched on debts. "I gave her very generous terms and a lower rate of interest than I would have for anyone else. This is how she repays me." Then, realizing what he'd said, he clarified, "Rather, this is how she doesn't repay me."

"Look, Roger. You have every right to be angry. But I'm telling you, Mama has suffered an emotional collapse. You know we lost Daddy about sixteen months ago, and she just never got over it." Laurell didn't know for certain that her mother's widowhood had anything to do with why she was in a psychiatric hospital. But if it would shortcut this unbearable boor, she was willing to play that card.

"Well, why didn't you say so in the beginning? I'm sure sorry to hear Cousin Myra's not well."

Laurell decided she should strike while she had the option. "So tell me, Roger, how much will it take, three payments and late fees, to square us away?" Then a troubling question occurred. "And when is the next payment due?"

As he threw out a number that made Laurell cringe, she was frantically thumbing through the B&B checkbook to see how much was in the inn's general account.

There's not enough here for more than two-thirds of that amount, and that would wipe us out.

"The next payment is due in nine days." He named the amount, and Laurel felt herself shrivel at the task of finding that much money.

No way around it. I'll have to dip into the life insurance money to make this happen. And I'm going ahead and make the next payment.

She knew with no guests, there wouldn't be income to cover the next payment. Better to do it this way and buy a little time.

"Give me your address. I know Mama has it here somewhere, but this will keep me from having to hunt it."

When he'd given her the information, and she'd verified the total amount needed, she said, "I will have a cashier's check in the mail to you today. And once you get it, we're not in danger of foreclosure. Right?"

"Not unless you fall behind again."

"Trust me," she said. "That will not happen."

Chapter Thirteen

"I 'm sorry, Miss Wilson, but if your mother is confined to a mental facility, we cannot honor her signature on any withdrawal document you might present." The speaker's lips pursed as if Laurell should have known before he added, "It's strictly against the law."

The words had come from the manager of the local branch of the investment bank that held Laurell's father's life insurance proceeds. Laurell had been honest and up-front about the situation. She had come there first, to be certain what would be needed to access the funds, and was ready to head to Asheville to secure Myra Wilson's authorization.

So much for honesty! I feel like I should have just gotten Mama's signature on a withdrawal slip and said nothing.

"But Mr. Baldwin," Laurell protested, all the while feeling the floor slipping out from under her. "Because of Mama's condition, she didn't pay the mortgage. I've promised the lien holder that a cashier's check will go out to them today." She knew her voice was taking on a pleading quality, but she didn't care. If it took begging and groveling, she would do that. "If I don't make that payment, we'll lose our home and our business. I have to have that money."

"I'm sorry," he said, although Laurell detected no true indication of regret in either his tone or his body language. "As soon as she's released and her doctor has certified her as being capable of managing her own business, come back to see us. We'll be glad to cut the check."

"Fat lot of good that will do," she said to Mrs. MacCallum, but loudly enough for the bank officer to hear. What's more, right at that moment, she didn't care if she came across as rude.

"Thank you for allowing us to serve your needs," the man said, before he turned on his heel and left them standing in the middle of the lobby.

Laurell was numb as she and her friend made their way to the van. "What am I going to do?" she wailed. "How am I supposed to pay all these other bills if I don't have access to our money?" It had suddenly dawned on her that her mother's signature was the only signature on all their accounts.

I'm so dead in the water. Doctors, lawyers, hospital and ambulance, and who knows what else? I can't pay any of them. I can't even hire an attorney for Russell. There's less than a thousand dollars in the B&B account, but I can't even write a check to get it.

"I'm calling Brother Bill," Mrs. MacCallum said, and grabbed for her phone. "Maybe he can advise us."

"By the time she ended the conversation, Laurell could already tell by her expression that there was no encouraging news.

"You need to petition the court for guardianship of your mother."

"That means another lawyer." She wiped her brow. "I can't pay the one we already owe."

"It means a lawyer, and it also means time you don't have. Brother Bill says the guardianship process can often take a month or more to work through."

"What am I going to do, Mrs. MacCallum? This is all so unfair. Mama just keeps saddling me with responsibilities that aren't mine."

"I think we need to talk to Mr. McComb again. Right now he's the only attorney we know." She put the van into motion, and before Laurell was ready to deal with it all, they were seated across from the lawyer.

"You need to know," Laurell told him, "I have no way right now to pay you for what you did yesterday, never mind anything else." She dropped her eyes, suddenly humiliated one too many times. "If you'd like for us to leave, I understand."

The attorney regarded her through tented fingers, before finally saying, "Why don't you tell me what's happening. We'll worry about payment later."

Aware that lawyers charged by the quarter hour, she made her explanation as short and concise as possible. "So you see, if I can't pay this mortgage arrearage, we'll lose the inn. Never mind paying all the other bills she's racking up right now. Mama's signature is the only one on all the bank accounts."

But if we get through this, it won't be that way any longer.

"Russell needs a lawyer, so they told me at the jail last night. I can't even do that."

"I'm really not worried about your brother," Mr. McComb said, although Laurell couldn't detect any rancor in his voice. "If there's no way to pay an attorney, then he can petition the court to appoint an attorney to represent him at no cost to him or you."

Laurell remembered seeing TV courtroom dramas where people were too poor to afford a lawyer. "Gosh, that would be a big load off my shoulders."

"Then you should inform the police this morning that all your mother's funds are frozen to you, and that they should arrange for your brother's representation."

"But what do I do about catching up the mortgage? There's so little time, and when I promised him this morning I'd get him a check, I never dreamed I couldn't make good."

"How much are we talking about?"

Laurell named the figure, then added, "That's three months, plus late charges, plus the next payment that's due in just over a week."

"And there's no one you could borrow from for a few weeks? I feel certain we could get a judge to grant you access to the money, but it can't happen overnight"

"That's not an option," she had to confess. "We don't have any family I can turn to."

"Then I'm afraid I can't help you, but neither am I going to charge you for anything I've done. I don't believe in kicking people while they're down."

"That's very generous of you," Laurell said. "Only what can I do? If I want to go to court, how do I go about that?"

"Before you start that process, why don't you talk to your mother's doctor and make him aware of your plight? There's every chance that she would be where her signature would be legal before the court process could work its course."

This is a lot of information to digest.

She and Mrs. MacCallum were back in the van, when Laurell said. "Take me to the jail please. Let me check on Russell and give them the news." Her brother had indeed been returned, Laurell learned. But she couldn't see him. He wasn't being a very cooperative prisoner, so there were no visitor privileges. Except his attorney. When she delivered the news that she couldn't afford that attorney, the facial reaction of the two officers spoke legions.

They've put us down as trash, but I can't be worried about it.

Back in the van, Mrs. MacCallum announced. "I've got a short-term solution to your problem."

"And that would be what?"

"I'm going to loan you enough to square away the inn." When Laurell began to protest, the woman held up her hand. "Hear me out. This is a loan. I can swing that. But you and I are going to reopen the inn."

"Do you think that's wise?"

"Look at it this way. If you redeem the mortgage but the place just sits there, what do you have? You'd be better off to save the money for your future and just let the guy foreclose."

"I shouldn't agree to this, but I can't bear the thought of us losing everything. We had a good business going until Mama started diverting income to pay for Russell's actions." She turned to her benefactor and said, "But do you think we can pull it off? There's a lot of work there."

"Sure," Mrs. MacCallum said, with more confidence than Laurell felt. "I'll move in there with you, and between the two of us, we'll make it work."

Laurell embraced her. "You will get your money back. I promise. I just can't believe you'd do all of this for me."

"There's a verse of scripture in the Book of Matthew where Jesus tells us that when we minister to others in need, it's like doing it for Him." She smiled at the uncomfortable young woman. "You have a need, I have a means to assist. God would have me do this."

"I never thought about God like that."

In truth, I've never thought much about God for anything. Mama always thought religion was a crutch for weak people.

In less than an hour they had visited Mrs. MacCallum's bank, and a check was in the post office on overnight delivery to satisfy the arrearage. Over burgers at one of the mom-and-pop restaurants that proclaimed it had the best burgers in North Carolina, the two women mapped out their actions.

"I wish I thought we could host guests tonight, but that would be unrealistic. Not that we have anyone wanting rooms."

"How do we find those people who do want rooms?"

Laurell found herself actually feeling confident about the task before them. Between what she'd absorbed from listening to her mother down through the years when she talked about the hospitality field, and the hands-on experience she'd gotten since coming to Hickory Bend, their game plan was already in her head. It just needed to be executed.

"First, we've got to get to the inn and do an assessment. Are we going back to serving lunch? Do we have any room reservations for the days ahead? Who have we disappointed by not being open after taking their reservation? How do we make amends?"

They returned to Oak Hill House, where Mrs. MacCallum had to disconnect the computer in Myra's office and bring it downstairs. In addition, she found a roll-away bed and set it up in a little storeroom near the kitchen that Laurell would use as a combination office and bedroom. It would still be a while before she could climb stairs. Fortunately, there was one full bath on the main level.

Mama could have come up with this same temporary solution. But she didn't.

Laurell reconnected the computer equipment and got online, while her partner made for the kitchen to inventory the food on hand and create a grocery list. Laurell was relieved to see that they had three reservations for two nights later. It was good fortune that all three reservations were for two nights each. Fearful that they might have heard by word of mouth that the inn was closed, she quickly dispatched emails telling each party how the B&B was looking forward to hosting them. By the time the day ended, she'd had responses from all three. They were equally anxious to arrive.

Next she put in a call to the director of the North Carolina B&B Association which also acted as a source for reservations and referrals. By the time she'd finished speaking with the woman she'd understood could be very aloof, Laurell believed she'd done as much damage control as possible.

"I'm so sorry Myra was taken suddenly ill. That's one of the downsides to being an innkeeper. When emergencies happen, there's often no backup."

"I was away when she got sick and was unable to travel myself." Laurell explained. "By the time I found out what was happening and got here, the inn had been closed for several days." She halted, took a deep breath, and said, "I know we've made some people mad, but it simply couldn't be helped."

"But you are open for business now?"

"We will re-open day after tomorrow."

"I'll spread the word," the woman said, and Laurell breathed a sigh of relief.

Her next order of business was to check in with Mrs. MacCallum, who reported that the kitchen would have to be restocked from scratch. "What little is left is spoiled or out of date, or there's so little, it's not worth counting."

"I guess that answers that question. We'll be doing good to be able to buy groceries for the afternoon guest socials and breakfast. We'd better hold off starting back the lunch business."

They agreed to make a shopping list and go the next morning to stock up, and Mrs. MacCallum assured her that she could underwrite the cost. "Next we've got to get all the guest rooms ready for occupancy."

She had put in a call to Phyllis, their housecleaning lady, who had unloaded all of her anger over how things had been handled, before refusing to return to work.

This bum leg business is getting old fast. Not being able to climb the stairs is really presenting a problem. Mrs. MacCallum can't make up the rooms without help. How are we going to do this?

Laurell returned to her temporary office and began pulling up the reservations of those people who had arrived and found the inn locked and unwelcoming.

I can't believe we lost revenue from at least forty-one room nights while we were closed. That's a lot of money that I could really use right now. Then reality hit. *But I couldn't have accessed it once it went into the checking account anyway.*

The need for money reminded her of the need to speak with her mother's doctor. She consulted the paperwork the local doctor had given her the previous afternoon, found the number for Dr. Jethro Penney, and dialed it. It took a few minutes for the doctor to be summoned to the phone. Laurell introduced herself and explained that she was Myra Wilson's daughter.

"If you're wanting to visit your mother," the doctor said, interrupting her spiel, "it's too soon."

"That's not why I'm calling," Laurell said quickly, lest he hang up. "I need to know how soon you think she will be recovered to the point that it's legal for her to sign checks and documents."

"I'm afraid I don't understand. We don't have anything to do with her personal business."

She tamped down her impatience and tried to explain where she'd found herself that morning. "We're penniless to run this business. I'm having to borrow money from friends to keep us going. But the attorney I spoke with this morning said that depending on her recovery, she might be legal to sign checks again before a court would have time to rule on my guardianship petition."

"I wish I could tell you she would be recovered enough in the next few days, but I don't want to give you unrealistic expectations. I'd say it'll be three weeks, and that's being very conservative. Your mother's been suffering for quite some time, and this won't be reversed overnight."

When Laurell ended the call she felt like the balloon that had suddenly been stuck with an unexpected straight pin. She hunted up her friend, whom she found upstairs taking stock of the bedrooms and making a list. Laurell had asked her to return to the ground floor so they could talk.

"We might as well forget trying to re-open," she shared. "The doctor says it will be at least three weeks before Mama can sign checks. We've got groceries to buy and utility bills to pay." Before she'd left the office, Laurell had scrounged in the file cabinet where Mama sometimes hid money and had found a little over a thousand dollars. She'd rolled it up and stuck it in her slacks pocket.

My fear is that even when she's legal to sign checks, she'll refuse to pull the money out to repay Mrs. MacCallum. If I give her most of this cash, that'll repay nearly half of what we owe her. But then we have no money on hand.

While they were debating whether they could get the inn reopened, the sound of cars coming into the yard alerted them to visitors.

"You stay here," Mrs. MacCallum said. "I'll see who it is." She checked the clock. "Isn't it a little early for guests wanting a room for the night?"

"It is," Laurell confirmed. "But people who don't already have a reservation will stop this early in case we don't have a vacancy and they need time to find other accommodations."

"We're not up for guests tonight, that's for sure. Those rooms up there need too much attention. I'll get rid of them, but I'll be polite."

Laurell found it humorous that her friend would make a point out of policing her behavior, but with all the concerns they had, she couldn't find the spirit to laugh.

"It's your mother's friend," Mrs. MacCallum announced, as she made her way back to where Laurell was sitting at her temporary desk. "She's brought your mother's car back."

Laurell struggled up from her chair and leaned on her walker to hobble to the foyer, where she met Wanda and another woman she didn't recognize.

Wanda approached, dangling a car fob from her finger. "Let me give you this right now. Otherwise, I'll put it in my purse, and none of us will ever see it again."

She hugged Laurell and greeted Mrs. MacCallum. "So how's it going, folks? How's Myra?"

Laurell brought their visitor up to date on her mother's condition, and added, "It will be at least a week, maybe longer, before I can visit her. The doctor says this breakdown has been coming on for a while."

"Myra never was the same after Richard died. I worked in the same office suite with her, and I know what I saw." She looked around. "This is a nice place. It's too bad this was just too much on top of everything else your mama was carrying. It's got the oomph that guests look for."

She surveyed the house again with the practiced eye of a hospitality professional and moved into the hall to explore the rest of the place. "You're re-opening. Right?"

Laurell didn't have the courage to admit that they were defeated, because saying it would make it true.

It was Mrs. MacCallum who answered the question. "Laurell was planning to reopen, but that may not happen."

"Why not? This inn should be a goldmine."

"It's a little thing called money," Laurell said at last. "Mama's the only one who can sign checks, and even if I could get to her, as long as she's in a mental hospital, her signature isn't legal." She spread her hands helplessly. "We have nothing to operate with."

"You're kidding. You can't sign on your mother's money?"

"It never occurred to me that I'd need to until this morning, when I went to spend some of Dad's insurance money and they denied me."

Wanda's face showed disgust. "I told Myra she needed to put you on the signature card, too. Tried to make her see that there needed to be more than one signature. Obviously, she didn't pay me any mind."

Don't feel bad, she didn't pay me any mind either. Wait a minute…

"Too? Did you say, too?"

"Yeah, I'm a co-signer on your mother's investment account. And you were supposed to be as well." She dropped her purse to the floor and collapsed into a chair nearby. "I never dreamed Myra didn't follow through, because I felt funny being an authorized signature." She looked at Laurell and her eyes gave the impression they were pleading for understanding.

"I'm not family. But Myra said she wanted somebody who wasn't related to her. I couldn't talk her out of it."

"So you're telling me that you can withdraw money from the insurance investment account?"

"I never have, but I signed all the papers at the branch bank in Atlanta, right after your mother got the insurance check."

"Oh, Wanda," Laurell exclaimed "you are a lifesaver! Let me tell you what we're up against."

For the next few minutes, Laurell went over everything that had happened.

"We've got three rooms reserved for tomorrow night, but without operating money, we're dead in the water." She hesitated, reluctant to even hope that this could go smoothly. "Are you willing to withdraw some funds from that account tomorrow? She outlined what had to be paid, emphasizing Mrs. MacCallum's role in getting the mortgage current.

"You know Mama well enough to know that she may not

appreciate us pulling out that money, but if we're going to reopen this week, we don't have any choice."

"Look, Myra messed up when she didn't put you on the account. If she gives me any grief, I'll put her in her place. I can do it, too." She looked at Mrs. MacCallum. "You will get your money back tomorrow, first thing."

Over the next hour, while Mrs. MacCallum drove to the village to pick up some basic supplies, Laurell and Wanda went over all that had to be paid and what needed to be purchased in order to operate for several days. Wanda provided several suggestions on how Laurell might reach out to those who were entitled to an apology.

"Be succinct. The innkeeper was suddenly taken ill and there was no one here to step in. You're so sorry for this inconvenience, and you'd like to offer them a complimentary night to compensate."

"A free night! Wanda, we had forty-one reservations that weren't honored. It'll bankrupt us."

Wanda laughed, then quickly sobered. "Don't panic," she said. "For starters, not all of them will take your offer. Most of them won't simply because it isn't convenient. Others will want to, but won't ever follow through. And those who do accept won't all come at the same time."

She reached to hug Laurell, to reassure her. "You've shouldered a mighty load all this time. Myra has abused you, and I hope when she gets better, she can see that."

"I guess we can afford to give away a room every so often in the name of good PR."

"Industry stats say that only about ten percent of those will actually accept. You're probably only looking at four or five rooms, at most."

"We can do that," Laurell said, feeling much relieved.

"Even those who don't take advantage of the free night will remember that they were offered a free night. You'll have left a good taste in their mouths."

When Mrs. MacCallum returned, she'd purchased enough groceries to put together a meal, and that was how, late in the evening, the four women sat around the island in the kitchen enjoying a home cooked meal. Wanda not only agreed to go with Laurell the next morning to the bank to get the money she needed, but she and her sister volunteered to forget their trip and stay to help.

"You've got an entire inn that needs a good cleaning. We can make that happen, and then after lunch day after tomorrow, we'll head back to Atlanta." She patted Laurell's hand. "That way, you and Mrs. MacCallum can tend to the nuts and bolts of being ready to open on time."

"If I could get up and move around, I'd come hug each of you." Laurell felt herself choking up, and struggled to maintain her composure. "There's no way I can ever thank you for all you've done."

"There's just one thing I want to know," Wanda said, as they were finishing their meal. "What are you doing about your art? That's another thing I may have to talk to Myra about. This young woman is too talented not to be studying and working," she said to her dinner companions.

Laurell hated to throw her mother under the bus, but she knew she had to answer honestly.

"Mama said we'd do something about art lessons, but it just never happened."

"It's going to happen now," Wanda vowed.

"You can say that again," Mrs. MacCallum said in echo. She looked at Laurell as if studying her internally. "You haven't said anything about what you read the other night."

The memory of all those scrapbook articles appeared in her mind's eye. "To be honest, I didn't know what to say. Then everything got so crazy, I hadn't thought any more about it."

"Say what?" Wanda asked. She looked from Laurell to Mrs. MacCallum and back.

Laurell in turn looked at the woman who had done so much for her. When she saw the slight nod of the older woman's head, she began.

"Mrs. MacCallum was at one time one of the most famous artists in this country. Thirty years ago her paintings were commanding thousands and thousands of dollars. Then tragedy struck, and she gave up her passion." She glanced at her friend. "Does that about sum it up, Mrs. MacCallum?"

"Nope," her friend said. "It's just the start of things." She looked at other three and said, "I gave up my passion, but this young woman isn't forsaking her passion, not as long as I have breath in my body."

"Bravo!" Wanda said, and clapped her hands.

As Laurell listened, she had to pinch herself. "Bravo, indeed!"

Mountain Laurell

One Year Later...

"Laurell, are you where you can come to the lobby?"

As she leaned into her easel, painting a small area of detail on the little church in the woods, where she now attended every Sunday, Laurell heard her mother's voice over the intercom. She crossed to the wall panel, pushed the talk button, and said, "Be right there."

It was still surprising when she heard the unexpected sound of her mother's voice. Until only a few weeks before, she'd been gone from the inn, serving a jail sentence for helping Russell escape.

I still don't think she's totally back with us.

She replaced her brush where it would be waiting, removed the old oversize shirt that she wore to paint, smoothed her hair, and left the attic space she'd converted into a studio. When she caught sight of the visitor waiting for her on the main level, her face broke into a smile.

"Brother Bill," she cried, and hurried to greet her pastor. "It's so good to see you."

"I know I probably disturbed your painting, but I need to run an idea by you."

"I can always take a break for you." She motioned toward the great room. "Let's sit in here where we can be comfortable."

As they settled into their seats, the pastor said, "You're looking good. And you're walking a lot better."

"Listen, there was a time when I seriously wondered if I'd ever be able to climb these stairs again."

"I'm in awe of you. You're a fighter, and I'm not just talking about your battle to recover from your broken leg."

He's talking about all the trouble with Russell, and Mama's breakdown and jail time, and us almost losing this lodge. It's been a very eventful year, that's for sure.

"So how are things going?"

Laurell didn't find his query out of line, because she knew, if it hadn't been for this young pastor and many members of his church, she might not have made it through the many black moments. For sure, she wouldn't have found the relationship with Jesus that had been missing from her life.

I didn't even know I was lost, until they all showed me.

"Things are going well." She glanced around the inn. "It's taken a while, but we've gradually built back our business. Most nights we're full, and some nights we even have to turn away people wanting a room."

"How's your mother?"

Ah, yes. Mother. How is she? Really?

"She's still going to therapy and on medication, but she's come a long way. If I could just get her to come to church with me. Despite spending time in jail, she still considers religion to be a crutch for the weak."

Mama's always been stiff and difficult. I see that now. But she still can't quite get it that she almost cost us everything. Some of her decisions and actions were downright stupid. Some of them were dangerous, and some were illegal. If anybody ever needed a crutch, it's her.

"Well," the preacher said, "we won't give up on her." He regarded Laurell with a knowing glance. "The best way you can reach her is by showing her how you're living as a Christian. Sooner or later, she'll want some of what you have."

"I hope so. I worry about her, and I'm very concerned about Russell."

"What's happening with him?"

"As you know, because Mama carried him back into Georgia, the probation sentence he got there, before we moved to North Carolina, was reinstated. He's serving a sentence here, and when he's done, he'll have to go back to Georgia and serve another sentence."

"Sounds rough. How's he dealing with all of that?"

How was he dealing? If the reports from the authorities were any indication, he wasn't doing well at all. "He's so angry, he keeps getting into trouble because he either can't or won't control himself." She sighed, heard it, and realized how dejected she sounded. "In truth, I wonder if he'll ever wise up and understand that he's his own worst enemy."

"That's a lesson he'll have to learn before he can learn anything else."

Laurell was suddenly weary of rehashing the problems of the past. "It's also a lesson that Mama's going to have to learn. But enough about us. What can I do for you this morning?"

There was no way she would ever want to be disrespectful to the man who had helped to save her twice. At the same time, a way to make her paintbrush create an aura that her painting needed had suddenly presented itself. She was anxious to get back to her easel before she forgot.

"As you know, we're holding Vacation Bible School later this summer. I was wondering if you would be willing to teach art to the kids. We'd like them to be able to finish a small painting in the five days we'll have."

"Well, sure. I could probably do that." Her mind was twirling as she tried to decide what questions she needed to ask.

As if he anticipated her concerns, Brother Bill said, "It'll be the first five days in August, and we'll probably have about twenty kids." At the look of horror on Laurell's face, he quickly added, "We'll supply all the materials, but you'll need to give me a list."

Laurell agreed, they talked for a few more minutes, and the preacher prepared to take his leave. "So how are you and Mrs. MacCallum making it these days?"

Mention of the friend and mentor who had opened so many doors made Laurell smile. "Except for my lessons three times a week, I rarely see her these days."

"I'm sure she's burning the candle at both ends, getting ready for that New York Gallery show in October."

"Oh, Brother Bill, you should see some of what she's turning out. It's like she never put down her brush."

"And I hear you're going to be a part of that same show."

She told me weeks ago, but I still can't believe I'm going to be hanging in a big, important New York show.

"I'm still pinching myself."

"Leave it to Mrs. MacCallum to think of others," the preacher said. "She believes in you, and from what little of your work I've seen, her confidence is well placed."

They parted company, and Laurell made her way back upstairs, her mind far away from the mountains of North Carolina. As anxious as she was to get back to her studio, her memory was calling up the gallery she'd visited with Mrs. MacCallum several months before. The same gallery where eight of her paintings would be hanging in the fall. It had been her first trip to New York, and as she'd stood in the massive, minimalist space and tried to visualize herself mixing with the art lovers who would be coming, a thrill had consumed her.

Stuff like this doesn't happen to Laurell Wilson.

She made her way back to the attic, suddenly desperate to feel the brush in her hand again. The first time she'd picked it up after such a long drought, it'd felt like a reunion with a long-lost friend. And when they'd been reunited, as she went back to work on the painting under construction, memories of how everything had fallen together to benefit her wouldn't leave her mind.

Mama had been hospitalized longer than even the doctor had estimated. The first time Laurell had been allowed to visit, Mrs. MacCallum had driven her to Asheville. Mama had shown no emotion at all when Laurell entered the room, and had proceeded to turn away from her.

It felt like a knife in my back. My mother didn't want to see me…

Conversation with the doctor afterward had assured Laurell

that she shouldn't take her mother's actions as a slam.

"Your mother simply isn't ready to re-associate with the world outside of herself. That's one of the reasons we asked you to come," Dr. Penney had explained. "We needed to see how she would react."

When she finally was released to come home, there had been an immediate set-back. Upon hearing that Russell was in prison and wouldn't be getting out any time soon, because of the many and various charges he faced, she'd suffered a relapse. Myra Wilson was returned to Asheville, where she stayed three more weeks, while Laurell and Mrs. MacCallum kept the inn operational and barely in the black.

Thanks to Wanda's rescue, Laurell had been able to tap into the investment money to pay the bills to keep them open. And on the second day after Myra finally came home to stay, on Wanda's insistence and with Dr. Penney's reinforcement, she had driven her mother to the bank, where Laurell's name was declared an authorized signature on all the accounts.

Mama wasn't very happy about it, and I don't think the bank manager was thrilled. But it was legal, and I've been able to sleep a lot sounder since then. That was also the first time I was able to drive.

Slowly, over time, the B&B clientele had returned, and the restoration of the daily lunch had proven most popular.

"It's a lot of work," Mrs. MacCallum had said one afternoon after an especially brutal midday business, "but it's a moneymaker."

"It's almost like I can't afford not to offer lunch."

When Myra returned from the hospital again, she was a ghost

of her former self and had been remanded to custody and served several months in the local jail. The judge had been compassionate and most lenient, Laurell knew, although Myra hadn't shared that opinion. Little of the woman who had once been an executive with a major hotel company remained. Wanda visited every few weeks, and that had been her assessment as well. Myra went through the motions, Laurel knew, but it was almost like she was a shell of her former self.

"You need to face facts," Wanda had said to Laurell in a private conversation. "Myra may never come back as we knew her. It could be this innkeeper role is too much for her now." Then she'd shaken her finger in Laurell's face. "But whether your mother comes back or not, you've wasted too much time taking care of her and not enough taking care of yourself."

Come to find out, Wanda and Mrs. MacCallum had been in conversation. Shortly after her conversation with Wanda, Laurell found herself taking one-on-one instruction from one of the nation's most famous but reclusive artists. Mrs. MacCallum, she had come to learn, was a Dr. Jekyll / Mr. Hyde personality when she was teaching. She was fair, but she was demanding, and she was tough.

I can easily understand how she became so famous. But the really wonderful news is that when I went back to painting, so did she.

It was going to be a professional resurrection to be remembered, the media reports said, when the announcement was first made that the artist, who had gone underground following tragedy so many years before, was mounting a comeback.

As thrilled as she was for her friend's good press, what Laurell hadn't expected was that she would be carried along on Mrs. MacCallum's coattails.

"My daughter was already a better artist than I could ever hope to be, and had the whole world waiting for her, when she was taken from me so cruelly." Mrs. MacCallum had voiced those words at a press conference at the gallery announcing her upcoming show. "Her loss was crippling, and I withdrew into myself and totally lost the desire to paint. I never again even touched a brush."

Laurell felt cold chills consume her, as she recalled yet again the words that had stunned her. When Mrs. MacCallum asked her to go along on the trip to New York, Laurell had assumed she would be nothing more than a travel companion. Standing there alongside her friend and the gallery owners and some more important people she didn't know, she'd been struck dumb at Mrs. MacCallum's next words.

"However, God has led me to a young woman who is every bit as talented as my precious Muriel was. She's as pretty, too. And because of her, I've been inspired to put brush to canvas. If it were not for Laurell Wilson, I wouldn't have found the inspiration to follow my passion again." She reached for Laurell's hand, smiled at her, and said, "That's why I've entered into an agreement with the Warnok Gallery to include a small hanging of Laurell's work along with mine."

A gasp went up from the crowd, but no one was more shocked than Laurell herself.

"I'll be honest," Mrs. MacCallum said, "I want the credit for discovering the young woman that I predict will set the nation's art world on its ear. Then I'm just going to stand in the wings and applaud and pat myself on the back."

Laurell had been certain that she was dreaming, that she would wake up and discover that none of the New York trip had actually happened. But the manner in which Mrs. MacCallum began to groom and direct her to be ready for her part of the show, had convinced her that it was all very real.

The other good part of the past few months had been coming to find Jesus. It had happened in the little church in the woods, where the members had embraced her and showed her by example how it was necessary to forgive and to serve others.

That's how I've been able to hug Mama, to tell her that I love her, and to forgive her for all the things that have hurt me. Mrs. MacCallum said once that when you hate someone else, you're actually the one who's poisoned and literally eaten alive.

Through the many friendships she made at church, she'd come to feel very much at home in Hickory Bend. There were friends, her age and older, that she hadn't had in Atlanta. In spite of her mother's many poor decisions, Laurell would vow that bringing them to a bed-and-breakfast inn deep in the mountains of North Carolina had been one of the best decisions Myra Wilson had ever made.

I found myself here. Literally.

During one of her many walks in the beautiful mountains that surrounded and cradled them, she'd discovered huge bushes that were a deep, beautiful green ten months out of the year. But in the spring, those same plants that literally grew wild in the mountains, burst into bloom with exquisite white flowers with red markings. She'd seen the blooms their first spring in the mountains, but it hadn't been until the most recent spring that she'd fallen in love with the petite blossoms.

"They're Mountain Laurel blooms," Mrs. MacCallum had explained. "Symbolically, they stand for ambition and perseverance, and they're just plain beautiful, besides. If you remember, the ancient Greeks awarded crowns of laurel leaves as a mark of accomplishment."

Laurell had learned about laurel wreaths in school, but never had she expected to encounter laurel out in the real world. The beauty of the plant and its flowers that spoke so eloquently stayed with her. Even in the coldest part of the winter, when snow lay several inches deep on the ground, she could still remember the many beautiful blooms that would flood the hills and valleys come spring.

When the New York show became reality, Mrs. MacCallum had said. "Many of the paintings in your bedroom will do nicely. But you really want to give some thought to at least two, perhaps three new pieces. Do you have any ideas?"

It hadn't taken but a second for Laurell to know exactly which pieces she wanted to create.

"The church," she said. "Definitely. I've been wanting to paint it since the very first time I saw it." She paused, stuck the tip of her pen in her mouth, then said, "The other, I think, should be those beautiful laurel blooms that scream the mountains.'"

"I think both of those subjects are good ones, and there's no doubt on my part that you can pull it off."

That was how it had begun. Because time was short, Laurell had actually set up two easels. Every day she worked on one, sometimes both pieces. Several times a week, her instructor and mentor was looking over her shoulder, critiquing, suggesting, and on rare occasions, giving what she was doing a thumb's down.

"The beauty of acrylic paint is that it cleans off and paints over easily. You don't have to live with a mistake."

"I never thought about it that way."

"Don't ever get sloppy in the name of finishing," Mrs. MacCallum said more than once. "I'd rather see you exhibit an incomplete piece before I'd let you hang something that wasn't as good as you are."

"Do you really think I'm that good?" She would ask.

"Wouldn't be squandering my valuable time if I didn't think your gift was worth developing." She would grin and add, "You're not the only artist hanging in that show, you know!" They would both laugh, but it would leave Laurell questioning yet again how she could have been so fortunate.

To think when I had to relinquish my scholarship that I thought my art career was finished. God really does work on His own timeline.

It had been a sermon by Brother Bill on the subject of waiting on God to do what He was going to do, never mind that it was on a different timeline, that had spoken to her. Laurell had sat in church that morning, feeling like the pastor was talking about her.

"I was having cold chills," she'd confided to Mrs. MacCallum afterwards. "How did Brother Bill know all about my past?"

"He probably doesn't know any specifics. But the Holy Spirit does, and that's how he knew what to say."

From that day on, Laurell had tried to clamp down her impatience. After all, she'd reasoned, if she was in college studying art, she wouldn't soon be mounting her part of a two-person show with one of the nation's foremost artists. But it had sure been hard to see all of that then.

"Which is why," Brother Bill had said when she talked with him about it later, "you have to proceed with faith that God's gonna do what God's gonna do." He grinned. "And He does it when it fits His plan."

"I'm beginning to see that," she'd confessed. "But sometimes I can't help but get impatient."

"You're not alone in that," the preacher said.

As the summer wound from Memorial Day to Labor Day, Laurell stayed busy. Between the demands of the B&B, including picking up wherever Myra dropped the ball, her work with church and time to paint, she found herself on the go from sunrise 'til very late in the evening. But the sense of fulfillment that she experienced more than compensated for the fatigue that dogged her daily.

Vacation Bible School came and went, and thirty-two children went home with finished paintings. Preparation had been made for two dozen children. Brother Bill had made a hasty run back to Asheville to purchase more supplies, so that on day two, every child could be painting. It had proven to be a most popular experience for both the kids and Laurell.

If this is how Mrs. MacCallum feels when she helps me succeed, now I understand why she does it!

The trees were beginning to take on their multi-colored hues, and every night, the inn was full with "leaf-lookers," as the autumnal tourists were known in the trade. After several long days of work, during which Laurell knew the inn had suffered, her two new paintings were finished.

Mama just won't step up to the plate and do any more than she's doing. Is this the new normal? I need to ask her doctor the next time she has an appointment.

Laurell had taken it upon herself several months back to hire some part-time people willing to work on an as-needed basis. She'd had to pay out more to get everything covered while she finished her paintings, but the work had gotten done. More importantly, the guests hadn't noticed.

Their paintings were being shipped by secured carrier, so the gallery staff could get the show organized and hung ahead of time. She and Mrs. MacCallum were flying up two days ahead of the opening reception. She had asked Mama if she would go as well, but had been politely informed that Myra wasn't comfortable leaving the state. Russell might need something.

Never mind that he's behind bars and not likely to need anything Mama could supply. One more time, I come in second.

Unlike previous times, her mother's dismissal of her needs didn't hurt. Laurell was beyond that point, and had no problem offering forgiveness, even though her mother hadn't asked to be forgiven.

I have bigger opportunities ahead. Maybe Russell does need Mama more than I do.

Their plane landed in New York, and a limousine was waiting to whisk them into the city. When she first glimpsed her paintings hung within sight of her mentor's many pieces, Laurell found her breath caught in her chest.

At the opening reception the next evening, when Laurell wore the gold lame' pants and gold and silver striped top that Wanda had selected and bought as a good-luck gift, she kept hearing one after another comment. Everyone was taken with the light effect that had somehow been infused into her paintings. An unbelievable glow, some called it.

"Look at this," she heard a woman say to her companion. "Look at how those windows just pull you in and make it where you can't resist coming inside."

Assuming that they were speaking of one of Mrs. MacCallum's pieces, Laurell turned in their direction.

It's the church. They're talking about MY church!

"Well, you know," the woman's companion said, "this young woman is Mary Elizabeth's protégé."

"Obviously, she's shared her technique that gives her paintings that inner light."

Laurell couldn't believe what she was hearing. She racked her brain, trying to remember if her mentor had ever mentioned that glow, that inner light.

This is the first time I've ever heard about this.

Over the course of the evening, Laurell heard those same comments and others equally complementary several times. It was a highlight of the night, when the same woman who had commented on the church purchased it for her home. The price it brought had stunned her.

By the end of the reception, almost two-thirds of Mrs.

270

MacCallum's pieces had been bought, and Laurell had sold almost every piece. She would return to Hickory Bend with a good sum of money, and with the mountain laurel painting. It had brought rave reviews as well, but no one had shown any interest in buying it.

Secretly, Laurell was elated it hadn't sold. She could paint another church, and probably would, but from a different angle. The laurel painting, on the other hand, was validation that she'd overcome and would continue to overcome. It was assurance that God would care and guide her on His timeline. She would look daily at the laurel painting to remind herself that God was in charge.

She'd shared that same sentiment with her mentor, as their plane left the ground in New York.

"Your talent comes from God," Mrs. MacCallum had said. "If you can walk with Him and always let Him lead, there's no limit to what you can accomplish."

Laurell turned those words over and over in her head as they neared the Asheville Airport. It was questionable if Mama was ever going to be strong enough to actually manage the B&B. It might be necessary to sell out. But she understood that would be okay, as long as they followed God's lead in making those decisions.

Just like her favorite mountain flowers, she could stand against adversity and come back again. God had promised that when she elected to live for Him.

Coming in 2019 - 2020

Revenge and Gravy

Maudeann Holcombe is the instigator of the community grapevine in Crabapple Cove, Georgia. It's a responsibility she sandwiches in between waiting tables at the Eat & Greet, where she feeds all manner of appetites. For Mags Gordon, real estate broker at Mountain Magic Realty by Mags, and unofficial, unlicensed, unsanctioned private detective, the server, who has never missed a meal herself, is as much a thorn in the side as she is the saving grace of Mags' reputation. When Maudeann is suddenly confronted by a visitor from her carefully-hidden past, and that visitor mysteriously turns up dead in a pan of homemade brown gravy, Maudeann quickly rises to the surface as prime suspect number one. Enter Mags and Carole, private eyes extraordinaire, who must set their mouths just right, if they plan to set their faithful server free.

Unwillingly Amish

When you marry someone, you marry their entire family. Constance "Connie" Miller knew this when she married the man of her dreams, who led her to believe that he had no family. After the "I do's," she discovers that he does indeed have family, and that he's also fully Amish, rebelling against his family and religion. When he ultimately demands that she live with him in his home community, conduct herself as a traditional Amish wife, and live a conventional Amish lifestyle, Connie feels her entire existence disappearing. Never mind that living the "plain" life is totally foreign to everything Connie has ever known, and the Amish religion flies in the face of the Christian faith Connie has embraced since childhood. Against a paralyzing sense of total betrayal, she must find her way with the help of the only God she has ever known, and be faithful to the vows she made on her wedding day, all without losing her husband or sight of herself.

2020 Christmas Collector Series
Embracing Moonshine for Christmas

Margie Crawford enjoys life in the ultra-wealthy Atlanta, Georgia suburb of Buckhead, where her own palatial mini-compound rubs shoulders with the crème of the city's elite. She's come a long way from her bare-bones upbringing, as the daughter of an illiterate moonshiner. When her mother dies and her daddy is jailed for his liquor-making, Margie and her siblings are consigned to the state's child welfare system. Fast forward many years, and Margie is married to a man predicted to be the state's next governor. While doing charity work at a homeless shelter, she encounters a young woman she realizes is her biological younger sister. To embrace the woman threatens her husband's political future. But Christmas is only days away and Margie must weigh her need to reunite with her biological roots over the damage she could do to her husband and her social status. How she does this and the fall-out from her actions comprises this heartwarming Christmas story.

Alive By Default

America's dynamic, but extremely polarizing First Lady is killed, when the presidential aircraft she's aboard is blown out of the sky over the nation's heartland. For White House correspondent Patti Hobgood, who missed the now ill-fated flight because of a bad batch of chicken salad, the queasiness in her gut is surmounted only by her suspicions of the official explanation of the tragedy. Patti's journalism background demands that she investigate, and when her journey circles through eastern European capitals and back to D.C.'s very back doorstep, the reporter soon learns why the First Lady is dead. And why she may get to question the deceased firsthand, unless she ceases all inquiry.

Blessings and Conflict

Victims of domestic violence and abuse are affected for life. This is a sad fact that Margaret Haywood embraced early on in the pages of **Hear My Cry, Paths of Judgment,** and **Lift up Mine Eyes**. As she fought her way out of the aftermath of the violence that marred and destroyed their entire family unit, she and each of her children, Brian, Sally and Jason, acted and reacted in drastically different ways. How have the scars of what each experienced affected and directed where each of these four people are today? In the pages of **Blessings and Conflict**, catch up with these captivating individuals that readers bonded with over thirteen years ago. See where each of them is today, and how the specter of violence has colored each of their lives.

Sentenced to Freedom

Kathryn McCormick has been paroled from federal prison, after serving fourteen years for a massive Ponzi scheme conviction. She feels she's more than paid her debt to society, but her victims, their families, and even her closest family members feel otherwise. She's ready to pick up the pieces of her life and go forward. But she's shocked to learn that saying and doing are two different things, and she actually craves to be back behind bars, where she could always depend on what was. She credits her faith in God for getting her through those long, lonely years. She believes He has forgiven her. But it isn't until she begins trying to function in a world totally without structure, when she's trying to forgive all those who refuse to forgive her, that she begins to truly find God, and to understand how utterly lost and adrift her soul is.

To receive notices on upcoming book releases,
email to: jswriter@bellsouth.net
Check out my web site: www.jshiverswriter.com
Like me on Facebook: JShivers Wordweaver

About the Author

John Shivers began writing for his hometown newspaper when he was only fourteen years old. As a lifelong wordsmith – some have called him a wordweaver – his byline has appeared in over forty Christian and secular publications, winning him seventeen professional awards.

Hear My Cry, his first novel, was published in 2005, and a dream of forty-four years was realized. **Mountain Laurell** is his eighteenth book. Fourteen of those books are Christian fiction, three are mysteries, and one is a mainstream novel. Additional titles in all three genres are in the planning stage.

John and his wife, Elizabeth, and Callum and Rosie, their beloved four-legged children, divide their time between Calhoun, Georgia and Magee, Mississippi, where his Shivers' roots are almost 200 years planted. Since the fall of 2018, he has served as lay pastor of three United Methodist congregations in Smith County, Mississippi.

When their schedule permits, John loves to slip away to the northeast Georgia mountains. It is there, and at their rural retreat in Mississippi, where he hears music of the heart and inspiration for much of his writing.

Made in the USA
Columbia, SC
07 July 2020

12364930R00167